Penguin Books
A Scandalous Woman and Other Stories

Edna O'Brien was born in the West of
Ireland and now lives in London with her
two sons. She has written *The Country Girls,
Girl with Green Eyes, Girls in Their Married
Bliss, August is a Wicked Month, Casualties
of Peace, The Love Object, A Pagan Place,
Zee and Co.* and *Night,* all published by
Penguin. (*The Country Girls, Girls in Their
Married Bliss* and *The Love Object* are all
available in Penguins in the U.S.A.)

D0050224

Edna O'Brien

A Scandalous Woman
and Other Stories

Penguin Books

Penguin Books Ltd, Harmondsworth,
Middlesex, England
Penguin Books Inc., 7110 Ambassador Road,
Baltimore, Maryland 21207, U.S.A.
Penguin Books Australia Ltd, Ringwood,
Victoria, Australia
Penguin Books Canada Ltd, 41 Steelcase Road West,
Markham, Ontario, Canada
Penguin Books (N.Z.) Ltd, 182–190 Wairau Road,
Auckland 10, New Zealand

This collection first published by Weidenfeld & Nicolson 1974
Published in Penguin Books 1976

With the exception of 'A Scandalous Woman', 'Honeymoon' and
'Sisters', all the stories in this book appeared originally in somewhat
different form in the *New Yorker*.
'Honeymoon' appeared originally in *Cosmopolitan*.

Made and printed in Great Britain by
Hazell Watson & Viney, Aylesbury, Bucks
Set in Linotype Baskerville

For Tony Rosslyn

'I assure you the world is not as amusing as we imagined.'

— *Les Liaisons Dangereuses*

Contents

A Scandalous Woman   9
Over   44
The Favourite   67
The Creature   85
Honeymoon   94
A Journey   103
Sisters   118
Love-Child   128
The House of my Dreams   135

A Scandalous Woman

Everyone in our village was unique and one or two of the girls were beautiful. There were others before and after but it was with Eily I was connected. Sometimes one finds oneself in the swim, one is wanted, one is favoured, one is privy, and then it happens, the destiny, and then it is over and one sits back and knows alas that it is someone else's turn.

Hers was the face of a madonna. She had brown hair, a great crop of it, fair skin and eyes that were as big and as soft and as transparent as ripe gooseberries. She was always a little out of breath and gasped when one approached, then embraced, and said 'darling'. That was when we met in secret. In front of her parents and others she was somewhat stubborn and withdrawn, and there was a story that when young she always lived under the table to escape her father's thrashings. For one Advent she thought of being a nun but that fizzled out and her chief interests became clothes and needlework. She helped on the farm and used not to be let out much, in the summer, because of all the extra work. She loved the main road with the cars and the bicycles and the buses, and had no interest at all in the sidecar that her parents used for conveyance. She would work like a horse to get to the main road before dark to see the passers-by. She was swift as a colt. My father never stopped praising this quality in her and put it down to muscle. It was well known that Eily and her family hid their shoes in a hedge near the road, so that they would have clean footwear when they went to Mass, or to market, or later on, in Eily's case, to the dress dance.

The dress dance in aid of the new mosaic altar marked her debut. She wore a georgette dress and court shoes threaded with silver and gold. The dress had come from America long before but had been re-styled by Eily, and during the week before the dance she was never to be seen without a bunch of pins in her mouth as she tried out some different fitting. Peter the Master, one of the local tyrants, stood inside the door with two or three of his cronies both to count the money and to survey the couples and comment on their clumsiness or on their dancing 'technique'. When Eily arrived in her tweed coat and said 'Evening gentlemen' no one passed any remark, but the moment she slipped off the coat and the transparency of the georgette plus her naked shoulders were revealed, Peter the Master spat into the palm of his hand and said didn't she strip a fine woman.

The locals were mesmerized. She was not off the floor once, and the more she danced the more fetching she became, and was saying 'ooh' and 'aah' as her partners spinned her round and round. Eventually one of the ladies in charge of the supper had to take her into the supper room and fan her with a bit of cardboard. I was let to look in the window, admiring the couples and the hanging streamers and the very handsome men in the orchestra with their sideburns and the striped suits. Then in the supper room where I had stolen to, Eily confided to me that something out of this world had taken place. Almost immediately after she was brought home by her sister Nuala.

Eily and Nuala always quarrelled – issues such as who would milk, or who would separate the milk, or who would draw water from the well, or who would churn, or who would bake bread. Usually Eily got the lighter tasks because of her breathlessness and her accomplishments with the needle. She was wonderful at knitting and could copy any stitch just from seeing it in a magazine or in a knitting pattern. I used to go over there to play and though they were older than me they used to beg me to come and bribe me with empty spools or scraps of cloth for my dolls. Sometimes we played hide and seek, sometimes we played families and gave ourselves posh names and posh jobs, and we used to paint each other with the dye from plants or blue bags and treat each other's faces as if they were palettes, and then laugh and marvel at the blues and indigos and pretend to be natives and do hula hula and eat dock leaves. Once Nuala made me cry by saying I was adopted and that my mother was not my real mother at all. Eily had to pacify me by spitting on dock leaves and putting them all over my face as a mask.

Nuala was happiest when someone was upset and almost always she trumped for playing hospital. She was doctor and Eily was nurse. Nuala liked to operate with a big black carving knife, and long before she commenced, she gloated over the method and over what tumours she was going to remove. She used to say that there would be nothing but a shell by the time she had finished, and that one wouldn't be able to have babies, or women's complaints ever. She had names for the female parts of one, Susies for the breasts, Florries for the stomach, and Matilda for lower down. She would sharpen and re-sharpen the knife on the steps, order Eily to get the hot water, the soap, to sterilize

11

the utensils and to have to hand a big winding
sheet.

Eily also had to don an apron, a white apron, that
formerly she had worn at cookery classes. The kettle
always took an age to boil on the open hearth, and very
often Nuala threw sugar on it to encourage the flame.
The two doors would be wide open, a bucket to one,
and a stone to the other. Nuala would be sharpening
the knife and humming 'Waltzing Matilda', the birds
would almost always be singing or chirruping, the dogs
would be outside on their hind quarters, snapping at
flies and I would be lying on the kitchen table terrified
and in a state of undress. Now and then, when I caught
Eily's eye she would raise hers to heaven as much as to
say 'you poor little mite' but she never contradicted
Nuala or disobeyed orders. Nuala would don her mask.
It was a bright red papier mâché mask that had been in
the house from the time when some mummers came on
the day of the Wren, got bitten by the dog, and lost
some of their regalia including the mask and a legging.
Before she commenced she let out a few dry, knowing
coughs, exactly imitating the doctor's dry, knowing
coughs. I shall never stop remembering those last few
seconds as she snapped the elastic band around the
back of her head, and said to Eily 'All set Nurse?'

For some reason I always looked upwards and backwards and therefore could see the dresser upside down,
and the contents of it. There was a whole row of jugs,
mostly white jugs with sepia designs of corn, or cattle,
or a couple toiling in the fields. The jugs hung on
hooks at the edge of the dresser and behind them were
the plates with ripe pears painted in the centre of each
one. But most beautiful of all were the little dessert
dishes of carnival glass, with their orange tints and

their scalloped edges. I used to say good-bye to them, and then it would be time to close eyes before the ordeal.

She never called it an operation, just an 'op', the same as the doctor did. I would feel the point of the knife like the point of a compass going around my scarcely formed breasts. My bodice would not be removed just lifted up. She would comment on what she saw and say 'interesting', or 'quite' or 'oh dearie me' as the case may be, and then when she got at the stomach she would always say 'tut tut tut' and 'what nasty business have we got here.' She would list the unwholesome things I had been eating, such as sherbet or rainbow toffees, hit the stomach with the flat of the knife and order two spoons of turpentine and three spoons of castor oil before commencing. These potions had then to be downed. Meanwhile Eily, as the considerate nurse, would be mopping the doctor's brow, handing extra implements such as sugar tongs, spoon or fork. The spoon was to flatten the tongue and make the patient say 'Aah'. Scabs or cuts would be regarded as nasty devils, and elastic marks a sign of iniquity. I would also have to make a general confession. I used to lie there praying that their mother would come home unexpectedly. It was always a Tuesday, the day their mother went to the market to sell things, to buy commodities and to draw her husband's pension. I used to wait for a sound from the dogs. They were vicious dogs and bit everyone except their owners, and on my arrival there I used to have to yell for Eily to come out and escort me past them.

All in all it was a woeful event but still I went each Tuesday, on the way home from school, and by the time their mother returned all would be over, and I would be sitting demurely by the fire, waiting to be offered a shop biscuit, which of course at first I made a great pretence of refusing.

Eily always conveyed me down the first field as far as the white gate, and though the dogs snarled and showed their teeth, they never tried biting once I was leaving. One evening, though it was nearly milking time, she came further and I thought it was to gather a few hazelnuts because there was a little tree between our boundary and theirs that was laden with them. You had only to shake the tree for the nuts to come tumbling down, and you had only to sit on the nearby wall, take one of the loose stones and crack away to your heart's content. They were just ripe, and they tasted young and clean, and helped as well to get all fur off the backs of the teeth. So we sat on the wall but Eily did not reach up and draw a branch and therefore a shower of nuts down. Instead she asked me what I thought of Romeo. He was a new bank clerk, a Protestant, and to me a right toff in his plus-fours with his white sports bicycle. The bicycle had a dynamo attached so that he was never without lights. He rode the bicycle with his body hunched forwards so that as she mentioned him I could see his snout and his lock of falling hair coming towards me on the road. He also distinguished himself by riding the bicycle into shops or hallways. In fact he was scarcely ever off it. It seems he had danced with her the night she wore the green georgette, and next day left a note in the hedge where she and her family kept their shoes. She said it was the grace of God that she had gone there first thing that morning otherwise the note might have come into someone else's hand. He had made an assignation for the following Sunday, and she did not know how she was going to get out of her house and under what excuse. At least Nuala was gone, back to Technical School where she was learning to be a domestic economy instructress, and my sisters had returned to the convent so that we were able to hatch it without the bother of them eavesdropping on us. I said yes that I would be her accomplice, without knowing what I was letting myself in for. On the Sunday I told my parents that I was going with Eily to visit a cousin of theirs, in the hospital, and she in turn told her parents that we were visiting a cousin of mine. We met at the white gate and both of us were peppering. She had an old black dirndl skirt which she slipped out of, and underneath was her cerise dress with the slits at the side. It was a most compromising garment. She wore a brooch at the bosom. Her mother's brooch, a plain flat gold pin with a little star in the centre, that shone feverishly. She took out her little gold flapjack and proceeded to dab powder on. The puff was dry so she removed the little muslin cover, made me hold it delicately while she dipped into the powder proper. It was ochre stuff and completely wrecked her complexion. Then she applied lipstick, wet her kiss curl and made me kneel down in the field and promise never ever to split.

We went towards the hospital, but instead of going up that dark cedar-lined avenue, we crossed over a field, nearly drowning ourselves in the swamp, and permanently stooping so as not to be sighted. I said we were like soldiers in a war and she said we should have worn green or brown as camouflage. Her bright bottom, bobbing up and down, could easily have been spotted by anyone going along the road. When we got to the thick of the woods Romeo was there. He looked very indifferent, his face forward, his head almost as low as the handlebars of the bicycle, and he surveyed us carefully as we approached. Then he let out a couple of whistles to let her know how welcome she was. She stood beside him, and I faced them and we all remarked what a fine evening it was. I could hardly believe my eyes when I saw his hand go round her waist, and then her dress crumpled as it was being raised up from the back, and though the two of them stood perfectly still, they were both looking at each other intently and making signs with their lips. Her dress was above the back of her knees. Eily began to get very flushed and he studied her face most carefully, asking if it was nice, nice. I was told by him to run along: 'Run along Junior,' was what he said. I went and adhered to the bark of a tree, eyes closed, fists closed, and every bit of me in a clinch. Not long after, Eily hollered and on the way home and walking very smartly she and I discussed growing pains and she said there were no such things but that it was all rheumatism.

So it continued Sunday after Sunday, with one holy day, Ascension Thursday, thrown in. We got wizard in our excuses – once it was to practise with the school choir, another time it was to teach the younger children how to receive Holy Communion, and once – this was our riskiest ploy – it was to get gooseberries from an old crank called Miss MacNamara. That proved to be dangerous because both our mothers were hoping for some, either for eating or stewing, and we had to say that Miss MacNamara was not home, whereupon they said weren't the bushes there anyhow with the gooseberries hanging off. For a moment I imagined that I had actually been there, in the little choked garden, with the bantam hens and the small mouldy bushes, weighed down with the big hairy gooseberries that were soft to the touch and that burst when you bit into them. We used to pray on the way home, say prayers and ejaculations, and very often when we leant against the grass bank while Eily donned her old skirt and her old canvas shoes, we said one or other of the mysteries of the Rosary. She had new shoes that were clogs really and that her mother had not seen. They were olive green and she bought them from a gypsy woman in return for a table cloth of her mother's, that she had stolen. It was a special cloth that had been sent all the way from Australia by a nun. She was a thief as well. One day all these sins would have to be reckoned with. I used to shudder at night when I went over the number of commandments we were both breaking, but I grieved more on her behalf, because she was breaking the worst one of all in those embraces and transactions with him. She never discussed him except to say that his middle name was Jack.

During those weeks my mother used to say I was pale and why wasn't I eating and why did I gargle so often with salt and water. These were forms of atonement to God. Even seeing her on Tuesdays was no longer the source of delight that it used to be. I was wracked. I used to say 'Is this a dagger which I see before me,' and recalled all the queer people around who had visions and suffered from delusions. The same would be our cruel cup. She flared up. 'Marry, did I or did I not love her?' Of course I loved her and would hang for her but she was asking me to do the two hardest things on earth – to disobey God, and my own mother. Often she took huff, swore that she would get someone else – usually Una my greatest rival – to play gooseberry for her, and be her dogsbody in her whole secret life. But then she would make up, and be waiting for me on the road as I came from school, and we would climb in over the wall that led to their fields, and we would link and discuss the possible excuse for the following Sunday. Once she suggested wearing the green georgette, and even I, who also lacked restraint in matters of dress, thought it would draw untoward attention to her, since it was a dance dress and since as Peter the Master said 'She looked stripped in it.' I said Mrs Bolan would smell a rat. Mrs Bolan was one of the many women who were always prowling and turning up at graveyards, or in the slate quarry to see if there were courting couples. She always said she was looking for stray turkeys or turkey eggs but in fact she had no fowl, and was known to tell tales to be calumnious and as a result, one temporary school teacher had to leave the neighbourhood, do a flit in the night, and did not even have time to get her shoes back from the cobblers. But Eily said that we would never be found out, that the god Cupid was on our side, and while I was with her I believed it.

I had a surprise a few evenings later. Eily was lying in wait for me on the way home from school. She peeped up over the wall, said 'yoo hoo' and then darted down again. I climbed over. She was wearing nothing under her dress since it was such a scorching day. We walked for a bit, then we flopped down against a cock of hay, the last one in the field, as the twenty-three other cocks had been brought in the day before. It looked a bit silly and was there only because of an accident, the mare had bolted, broke away from the

hay cart and nearly strangled the driver, who was himself an idiot and whose chin was permanently smeared
with spittle. She said to close my eyes, open my hand
and see what God would give me. There are moments
in life when the pleasure is more than one can bear,
and one descends willy nilly into a wild tunnel of
flounder and vertigo. It happens on swing boats and
chairoplanes, it happens maybe at waterfalls, it is said
to happen to some when they fall in love, but it happened to me that day, propped against the cock of hay,
the sun shining, a breeze commencing, the clouds like
cruisers in the heavens on their way to some distant
port. I had closed my eyes, and then the cold thing hit
the palm of my hand, fitting it exactly, and my fingers
came over it to further the hold on it, and to guess what
it was. I did not dare say in case I should be wrong. It
was of course a little bottle, with a screw-on cap, and a
label adhering to one side, but it was too much to hope
that it would be my favourite perfume, the one called
'Mischief'. She was urging me to guess. I feared that it
might be an empty bottle, though such a gift would not
be wholly unwelcome, since the remains of the smell
always lingered; or that it might be a cheaper perfume,
a less mysterious one named after a carnation or a
poppy, a perfume that did not send shivers of joy down
my throat and through my swallow to my very heart.
At last I opened my eyes, and there it was, my most
prized thing, in a little dark blue bottle, with a sil-
verish label and a little rubber stopper, and inside, the
precious stuff itself. I unscrewed the cap, lifted off the
little rubber top and a drop of the precious stuff was
assigned to the flat of my finger and then conveyed to
a particular spot in the hollow behind the left ear. She
did exactly the same and we kissed each other and

breathed in the rapturous smell. The smell of hay intervened so we ran to where there was no hay and
kissed again. That moment had an air of mystery and
sanctity about it, what with the surprise and our
speechlessness, and a realization somewhere in the
back of my mind that we were engaged in rotten business indeed, and that our larking days were over.

If things went well my mother had a saying that it
was all too good to be true. It proved prophetic the
following Saturday because as my hair was being
washed at the kitchen table, Eily arrived and sat at the
end of the table and kept snapping her fingers in my
direction. When I looked up from my expanse of suds
I saw that she was on the verge of tears and was blotchy
all over. My mother almost scalded me, because in wel-
coming Eily she had forgotten to add the cold water to
the pot of boiling water and I screamed and leapt about
the kitchen shouting hellfire and purgatory. Afterwards Eily and I went around to the front of the house,
sat on the step where she told me that all was U.P. She
had gone to him as was her wont, under the bridge,
where he did a spot of fishing each Friday and he told
her to make herself scarce. She refused, whereupon he
moved downstream and the moment she followed he
waded into the water. He kept telling her to beat it,
beat it. She sat on the little milk stool, where he in fact
had been sitting, then he did a terrible thing which
was to cast his rod in her direction and almost remove
one of her eyes with the nasty hook. She burst into
tears and I began to plait her hair for comfort's sake.
She swore that she would throw herself in the self-same
river before the night was out, then said it was only a
lovers' quarrel, then said that he would have to see

her, and finally announced that her heart was utterly broken, in smithereens. I had the little bottle of perfume in my pocket, and I held it up to the light to show how sparing I had been with it, but she was interested in nothing only the ways and means of recovering him, or then again of taking her own life. Apart from drowning she considered hanging, the intake of a bottle of Jeyes Fluid, or a few of the grains of strychnine that her father had for foxes.

Her father was a very gruff man who never spoke to the family except to order his meals and to tell the girls to mind their books. He himself had never gone to school but had great acumen in the buying and selling of cattle and sheep, and put that down to the fact that he had met the scholars. He was an old man with an atrocious temper, and once on a fair day had ripped the clothing off an auctioneer who tried to diddle him over the price of an Aladdin lamp.

My mother came to sit with us, and this alarmed me since my mother never took the time to sit, either indoors or outdoors. She began to talk to Eily about knitting, about a new tweedex wool, asking if she secured some would Eily help her knit a three-quarter length jacket. Eily had knitted lots of things for us including the dress I was wearing – a salmon pink, with scalloped edges and a border of white angora decorating those edges. At that very second as I had the angora to my face tickling it, my mother said to Eily that once she had gone to a fortune teller, had removed her wedding ring as a decoy, and when the fortune teller asked was she married, she had replied no, whereupon the fortune teller said 'How come you have four children?' My mother said they were uncanny, those ladies, with their gypsy blood and their clairvoyant powers. I guessed exactly what Eily was thinking. Could we find a fortune teller or a witch who could predict her future?

There was a witch twenty miles away who ran a public house and who was notorious, but who only took people on a whim. When my mother ran off to see if it was a fox because of the racket in the henhouse I said to Eily that instead of consulting a witch we ought first to resort to other things, such as novenas, putting wedding cake under our pillows or gathering bottles of dew in the early morning and putting them in a certain fort to make a wish. Anyhow how could we get to a village twenty miles away, unless it was on foot or by bicycle, and neither of us had a machine. Nevertheless, the following Sunday, we were to be found setting off with a bottle of tea, a little puncture kit, and eight shillings, which was all the money we managed to scrape together.

We were not long started when Eily complained of feeling weak, and suddenly the bicycle was wobbling all over the road and she came a cropper as she tried to slow it down, by heading for a grass bank. Her brakes were non-existent as indeed were mine. They were borrowed bicycles. I had to use the same method to dismount, and the two of us with our front wheels wedged into the bank, and our handlebars askew, caused a passing motorist to call out that we were a right pair of Mohawks and a danger to the county council.

I gave her a sup of tea, and forced on her one of the eggs which we had stolen from various nests, and which were intended as a bribe for our witch. Along with the eggs we had a little flitch of home-cured bacon. She cracked it on the handlebars, and with much persuasion from me swallowed it whole, saying it was worse than castor oil. It being Sunday, she recalled other Sundays and where she would be at that exact moment and she prayed to St Anthony to please bring him back. We had heard that he went to Limerick most weekends now, and there was rumour that he was going out with a bacon curer's daughter, and that they were getting engaged.

The woman who opened the side door of the pub, said that the witch did not live there any longer. She was very cross, had eyebrows that met, and these as well as the hairs in her head were a yellowish grey. She told us to leave her threshold at once, and how dare we intrude upon her Sunday leisure. She closed the door in our faces. I said to Eily 'That's her.' And just as we were screwing up our courage to knock again, she re-opened the door and said who in the name of Jacob had sent us. I said we'd come a long way, miles and miles, I showed the eggs and the bacon in its dusting of salt-petre, and she said she was extremely busy, seeing as it was her birthday and that sons and daughters and cousins were coming for a high tea. She opened and closed the door numerous times, and through it all we stood our ground, until finally we were brought in, but it was my fortune she wanted to tell. The kitchen was tiny and stuffy, and the same linoleum was on the floor as on the little wobbling table. There was a little wooden armchair for her, a form for visitors and a stove that was smoking. Two rhubarb tarts were cooling on top, and that plus a card were the only indications of a birthday celebration. A small man, her husband, excused himself and wedged sideways through another door. I pleaded with her to take Eily rather than me, and after much dithering, and even going out to the garden to empty tea leaves, she said that maybe she would, but that we were pests the pair of us. I was sent to join her husband, in the little pantry, and was nearly smothered from the puffing of his pipe. There was also a strong smell of flour, and no furniture except a sewing machine with a half-finished garment, a shift, wedged in under the needle. He talked in a whisper, said that Mau Mau would come to Ireland, and that St Columbus would rise from his grave, to make it once again the island of saints and scholars. I was certain that I would suffocate. But it was worth it. Eily was jubilant. Things could not have been better. The witch had not only seen his initial, J, but seen it twice in a concoction that she had done with the whites of one of the eggs and some gruel. Yes things had been bad very bad, there had been grievous misunderstandings, but all was to be changed, and leaning across the table she said to Eily 'Ah sure, you'll end your days with him.'

Cycling home was a joy, we spinned downhill, saying to hell with safety, to hell with brakes, saluted strangers, admired all the little cottages and the outhouses and the milk tanks and the whining mongrels, and had no nerves passing the haunted house. In fact we would have liked to see an apparition on that most buoyant of days. When we got to the cross roads, that led to our own village, Eily had a strong presentiment, as indeed had I, that he would be there waiting for us, contrite, in a hair shirt, on bended knees. But he was not. There was the usual crowd of lads playing pitch and toss. A couple of the younger ones tried to impede us by standing in front of the bikes and Eily blushed red. She was a favourite with everyone that summer, and she had a different dress for every day of the week. She was called a fashion plate. We said good night and knew that it did not matter, that though he had not been waiting for us, before long he and Eily would be united. She resolved to be patient and be a little haughty and not seek him out.

Three weeks later, on a Saturday night, my mother was soaking her feet in a mixture of warm water and washing soda, when a rap came on the scullery window. We both trembled. There was a madman who had taken up residence in a bog-hole and we were certain that it must be him. 'Call your father,' she said. My father had gone to bed in a huff, because she had given him a boiled egg instead of a fry for his tea. I didn't want to leave her alone and unattended so I yelled up to my father, and at the same time a second assault was delivered on the window pane. I heard the words 'Sir, Sir'.

It was Eily's father, since he was the only person who called my father Sir. When we opened the door to him the first thing I saw was the slash hook in his hand, and then the condition of his hair which was upstanding and wild. He said 'I'll hang, draw, and quarter him,' and my mother said 'Come in Mr Hogan,' not knowing who this graphic fate was intended for. He said he had found his daughter in the lime kiln, with the bank clerk, in the most satanic position, with her belly showing.

My first thought was one of delight at their reunion, and then I felt piqued that Eily hadn't told me but had chosen instead to meet him at night in that disused kiln that reeked of damp. Better the woods I thought and the call of the cuckoo, and myself keeping some kind of watch, though invariably glued to the bark of a tree.

He said he had come to fetch a lantern, to follow them as they had scattered in different directions, and he did not know which of them to kill first. My father, whose good humour was restored by this sudden and unexpected intrusion, said to hold on for a moment, to step inside and that they would consider a plan of campaign. Mr Hogan left his cap on the step, a thing he always did, and my mother begged of him to bring it in, since the new pup ate every article of clothing that it could find. Only that very morning my mother looked out on the field and thought it was flakes of snow, but in fact it was her line of washing, chewed to pieces. He refused to bring in his cap which to me was a perfect example of how stubborn he was, and how awkward things were going to be. At once, my father ordered my mother to make tea, and though still gruff, there was between them now an understanding, because of the worse tragedy that loomed. My mother seemed the most perturbed, made a hopeless cup of tea, cut the bread in agricultural hunks, and did everything wrong as if she herself had just been found out in some base transaction. After the men had gone out on their search party, she got me to go down on my knees to pray with her, and I found it hard to pray because I was already thinking of the flogging I would get for being implicated. She cross-examined me. Did I know anything about it? Had Eily ever met him? Why had she made herself so much style, especially that slit skirt.

I said no to everything. These noes were much too hastily delivered, and only that my mother was so busy cogitating and surmising, she would have suspected something for sure. Kneeling there I saw them trace every movement of ours, get bits of information from this one and that one, the so-called cousins, the woman who had promised us the gooseberries, and Mrs Bolan. I knew we had no hope. Eily! Her most precious thing was gone, her jewel. The inside of one was like a little watch and once the jewel or jewels were gone the outside was nothing but a sham. I saw her die in the cold lime kiln and then again in a sick room, and then stretched out on an operating table the very way that I used to be. She had joined that small sodality of scandalous women who had conceived children without securing fathers and who were damned in body and soul. Had they convened they would have been a band of seven or eight, and might have sent up an unholy wail to their maker and their covert seducers. The one thing I could not endure was the thought of her stomach protuberant, and a baby coming out saying 'ba ba'. Had I had the chance to see her I should have suggested that we run away with gypsies.

Poor Eily, from then on she was kept under lock and key, and allowed out only to Mass, and then so concealed was she, with a mantilla over her face that she was not even able to make a lip sign to me. Never did she look so beautiful as those subsequent Sundays in chapel, her hair and her face veiled, her eyes like smoking tragedies peering through. I once sat directly in front of her, and when we stood up for the first gospel, I stared up into her face, and got such a dig in the ribs from my mother that I toppled over.

A mission commenced the following week, and a strange priest with a beautiful accent, and a strong sense of rhetoric, delivered the sermons each evening. It was better than a theatre – the chapel in a state of hush, scores of candles like running stairways, all lit,

27

extra flowers on the altar, a medley of smells, the white linen, and the place so packed that we youngsters had to sit on the altar steps and saw everything clearer, including the priest's adam's apple as it bobbed up and down. Always I could sight Eily, hemmed in by her mother, and some other old woman, pale and impassive, and I was certain that she was about to die. On the evening that the sermon centred on the sixth commandment, we youngsters were kept outside until Benediction time. We spent the time wandering through the stalls, looking at the tiers of rosary beads that were as dazzling as necklaces, all hanging side by side and quivering in the breeze, all colours, and of different stones, then of course the bright scapulars, and all kinds of little medals and beautiful crucifixes that were bigger than the girth of one's hand, and even some that had a little cavity within, where a relic was contained, and also beautiful prayer books and missals, some with gold edging and little holdalls made of filigree.

When we trooped in for the Benediction Eily slipped me a holy picture. It said 'Remembrance is all I ask, but if Remembrance should prove a task Forget me.' I was musing on it and swallowing back my tears at the very moment that Eily began to retch, and was hefted out by four of the men. They bore her aloft as if she was a corpse on a litter. I said to my mother that most likely Eily would die and my mother said if only such a solution could occur. My mother already knew. The next evening Eily was in our house, in the front room, and though I was not admitted, I listened at the door, and ran off only when there was a scream or a blow or a thud. She was being questioned about each and every event, and about the bank clerk and what exactly were her associations with him. She said no, over and over again, and at moments was quite defiant, and as they said an 'upstart'. One minute they were asking her kindly, another minute they were heckling, another minute her father swore that it was to the lunatic asylum that she would be sent, and then at once her mother was condemning her for not having milked for two weeks.

They were contrariness itself. How could she have milked since she was locked in the room off the kitchen, where they stowed the oats and which was teeming with mice. I knew for a fact that her meals – a hunk of bread and a mug of weak tea – were handed into her, twice a day, and that she had nothing else to do only cry, and think, and sit herself upon the oats and run her fingers through it, and probably have to keep making noises to frighten off the mice. When they were examining her my mother was the most reasonable but also the most exacting. My mother would ask such things as 'Where did you meet? How long were you together, were others present?' Eily denied ever having met him and was spry enough to say 'What do you take me for, Mrs Brady, a hussy?' But that incurred some sort of a belt from her father, because I heard my mother say that there was no need to resort to savagery. I almost swooned when on the glass panel of our hall door I saw a shadow, then knuckles, and through the glass the appearance of a brown habit, such as the missioner wore.

He saw Eily alone, and we all waited in the kitchen, the men supping tea, my mother segmenting a grapefruit to offer to the priest. It seemed odd fare to give him in the evening, but she was used to entertaining priests only at breakfast time, when one came every five or ten years to say Mass in the house to re-bless it, and put paid to the handiwork of the devil. When he was leaving, the missioner shook hands with each of us, then patted my hair, and watching his sallow face and his rimless spectacles, and drinking in his beautiful speaking voice, thought that if I were Eily I would prefer him to the bank clerk, and would do anything to get to be in his company.

I had one second with Eily, while they all trooped out to open the gate for the priest, and to wave him off. She said for God's sake not to split on her. Then she was taken upstairs by my mother, and when they re-emerged Eily was wearing one of my mother's mackintoshes, a Mrs Miniver hat, and a pair of old sunglasses. It was a form of disguise since they were setting out on a journey. Eily's father wanted to put a halter round her but my mother said it wasn't the Middle Ages. I was enjoined to wash cups and saucers, to empty the ashtray, and plump the cushions again, but once they were gone I was unable to move because of a dreadful pain that gripped the lower part of my back and stomach, and I was convinced that I too was having a baby and that if I were to move or part my legs some terrible thing would come ushering out.

The following morning Eily's father went to the bank, where he broke two glass panels, sent coins flying about the place, assaulted the bank manager, and tried to saw off part of the bank clerk's anatomy. The two customers – the butcher and the undertaker – had to intervene, and the lady clerk who was in the cloakroom managed to get to the telephone to call the barracks. When the Sergeant came on the scene, Eily's father was being held down, his hands tied with a skipping rope, but he was still trying to aim a kick at the blackguard who had ruined his daughter. Very quickly the Sergeant got the gist of things. It was agreed that Jack, that was the culprit's name, would come to their house that evening. Though the whole occasion was to be fraught with misfortune, my mother upon hearing of it, said some sort of buffet would have to be considered.

It proved to be an arduous day. The oats had to be shovelled out of the room and the women were left to do it, since my father was busy seeing the solicitor and the priest, and Eily's father remained in the town and boasting about what he wouldn't have done to the bugger only for the Sergeant coming on the scene.

Eily was silence itself. She didn't even smile at me when I brought the basket of groceries that her mother had sent me to fetch. Her mother kept referring to the fact that they would never provide bricks and mortar for the new house now. For years she and her husband had been skimping and saving, intending to build a house, two fields nearer the road. It was to be identical to their own house, that is to say a cement two-storey house, but with the addition of a lavatory, and a tiny hall inside the front door, so that, as she said, if company came, they could be vetted there instead of plunging straight into the kitchen. She was a backward woman and probably because of living in the fields she had no friends, and had never stepped inside anyone else's door. She always washed out of doors at the rain barrel, and never called her husband anything but Mister. Unpacking the groceries she said that it was a pity to waste them on him, and the only indulgence she permitted herself was to smell these things, especially the packet of raspberry and custard biscuits. There was blackcurrant jam, a Scribona swiss roll, a tin of herrings in tomato sauce, a loaf, and a large tin of fruit cocktail.

Eily kept whitening and re-whitening her buckskin shoes. No sooner were they out on the window than she would bring them in and whiten again. The women were in the room putting the oats into sacks. They didn't have much to say. My mother used always to laugh because when they met Mrs Hogan used to say 'any newses' and look up at her, with that wild stare, opening her mouth to show the big gaps between her front teeth, but the 'newses' had at last come to her own door, and though she must have minded dreadfully she seemed vexed more than ashamed, as if it was inconvenience rather than disgrace that had hit her. But from that day on she almost stopped calling Eily by her pet name which was Babbie.

I said to Eily that if she liked we could make toffee, because making toffee always humoured her. She pretended not to hear. Even to her mother she refused to speak, and when asked a question she bared her teeth like one of the dogs. She even wanted one of the dogs, Spot, to bite me, and led him to me by the ear, but he was more interested in a sheep's head that I had brought from the town. It was an arduous day, what with carting out the oats in cans and buckets, and refilling it into sacks, moving a table in there and tea chests, finding suitable covers for them, laying the table properly, getting rid of all the cobwebs in the corners, sweeping up the soot that had fallen down the chimney, and even running up a little curtain. Eily had to hem it and as she sat outside the back door I could see her face and her expression and she looked very stubborn and not nearly so amenable as before. My mother provided a roast chicken, some pickles and freshly boiled beets. She skinned the hot beets with her hands and said 'Ah you've made your bed now' but Eily gave no evidence of having heard. She simply washed her face in the aluminium basin, combed her hair severely back, put on her whitened shoes, and then turned around to make sure that the seams of her stockings were straight. Her father came home drunk, and he looked like a younger man trotting up the fields in his oatmeal-coloured socks – he'd lost his shoes. When he saw the sitting-room that had up to then been the oats room, he exclaimed, took off his hat to it and said 'Am I in my own house at all mister?' My father arrived full of important news which as he kept saying he would discuss later. We waited in a ring, seated around the fire, and the odd words said were said only by the men and then without any point. They discussed a beast that had had some ailment.

The dogs were the first to let us know. We all jumped up and looked through the window. The bank clerk was coming on foot, and my mother said to look at that swagger, and wasn't it the swagger of a hobo. Eily ran to look in the mirror that was fixed to the window ledge. For some extraordinary reason my father went out to meet him and straight away produced a packet of cigarettes. The two of them came in smoking, and he was shown to the sitting-room which was directly inside the door to the left. There were no drinks on offer since the women decided that the men might only get obstreperous. Eily's father kept pointing to the glories of the room, and lifted up a bit of cretonne, to make sure that it was a tea chest underneath, and not a piece of pricey mahogany. My father said 'Well Mr Jacksie, you'll have to do your duty by her and make an honest woman of her.' Eily was standing by the window looking out at the oncoming dark. The bank clerk said 'Why so' and whistled in a way that I had heard him whistle in the past. He did not seem put out. I was afraid that on impulse he might rush over and put his hands somewhere on Eily's person. Eily's father mortified us all by saying she had a porker in her, and the bank clerk said so had many a lass, whereupon he got a slap across the face, and was told to sit down and behave himself.

From that moment on he must have realized he was lost. On all other occasions I had seen him wear a khaki jacket and plus-fours, but that evening he wore a brown suit that gave him a certain air of reliability and dullness. He didn't say a word to Eily, or even look in her direction, as she sat on a little stool staring out the window and biting on the little lavalier that she wore around her neck. My father said he had been pup enough and the only thing to do was to own up to it, and marry her. The bank clerk put forward three objections – one that he had no house, two that he had no money, and three that he was not considering marrying. During the supper Eily's mother refused to sit down, and stayed in the kitchen nursing the big tin of fruit cocktail, and having feeble jabs at it with the old iron tin opener. She talked aloud to herself about the folks 'hither' in the room and what a sorry pass things had come to. As usual my mother ate only the pope's nose, and served the men the breasts of chicken. Matters changed every other second, they were polite to him remembering his status as a bank clerk, then they were asking him what kind of crops grew in his part of the country, and then again they would refer to him as if he was not there saying 'The pup likes his bit of meat.' He was told that he would marry her on the Wednesday week, that he was being transferred from the bank, that he would go with his new wife and take rooms in a midland town. He just shrugged and I was thinking that he would probably vanish on the morrow but I didn't know that they had alerted everyone, and that when he did in fact try to leave at dawn the following morning, three strong men impeded him and brought him up the mountain for a drive in their lorry. For a week after he was indisposed, and it is said that his black eyes were as big as bubble gum. It left a permanent hole in his lower cheek as if a little pebble of flesh had been tweezed out of him.

Anyhow they discussed the practicalities of the wedding while they ate their fruit cocktail. It was served in the little carnival dishes and I thought of the numerous operations that Nuala had done, and how if it was left to Eily and me that things would not be nearly so crucial. I did not want her to have to marry him and I almost blurted that out. But the plans were going ahead, he was being told that it would cost him ten pounds, that it would be in the sacristy of the Catholic church, since he was a Protestant and there were to be no guests except those present, and Eily's former teacher a Miss Melody. Even her sister Nuala was not going to be told until after the event. They kept asking him was that clear, and he kept saying 'Oh yeh,' as if it were a simple matter of whether he would have more fruit cocktail or not. The number of cherries were few and far between, and for some reason had a faint mauve hue to them. I got one and my mother passed me hers. Eily ate well but listlessly, as if she weren't there at all. Towards the end my father sang 'Master Mc-

Grath', a song about a greyhound, and Mr Hogan told
the ghost story about seeing the headless liveried man
at a cross roads, when he was a boy.

Going down the field Eily was told to walk on ahead
with her intended, probably so that she could discuss
her trousseau or any last-minute things. The stars were
never so bright or so numerous, and the moonlight cast
as white a glow as if it were morning and the world
was veiled with frost. Eily and he walked in utter
silence. At last, she looked up at him, and said something, and all he did was to draw away from her, and
there was such a distance between them as a cart or a
car could pass through. She edged a little to the right
to get nearer, and as she did he moved further away so
that eventually she was on the edge of a path and he
was right in by the hedge hitting the bushes with a bit
of a stick he had picked up. We followed behind, the
grown-ups discussing whether or not it would rain the
next day, but no doubt wondering what Eily had tried
to say to him.

They met twice more before the wedding, once in
the sitting-room of the hotel, when the travelling solicitor drew up the papers guaranteeing her a dowry of
two hundred pounds, and once in the city when he was
sent with her to the jewellers to buy a wedding ring.
It was the same city as where he had been seeing the
bacon curer's daughter and Eily said that in the jewellers he expressed the wish that she would drop dead. At
the wedding breakfast itself there were only sighs and
tears, and the teacher as was her wont stood in front of
the fire, and mindless of the mixed company hitched up
her dress behind, the better to warm the cheeks of her

bottom. In his giving away speech my father said they had only to make the best of it. Eily snivelled, her mother wept and wept and said 'Oh Babbie, Babbie', and the groom said 'Once bitten twice shy.' The reception was in their new lodgings, and my mother said that she thought it was bad form the way the landlady included herself in the proceedings. My mother also said that their household utensils were pathetic, two forks, two knives, two spoons, an old kettle, an egg saucepan, a primus, and as she said not even a nice enamel bin for the bread but a rusted biscuit tin. When they came to leave Eily tried to dart into the back of the car, tried it more than once, just like an animal trying to get back to its lair.

On returning home my mother let me put on her lipstick, and praised me untowardly for being such a good, such a pure little girl and never did I feel so guilty because of the leading part I had played in Eily's romance. The only thing that my mother had eaten at the wedding was a jelly made with milk. We tried it the following Sunday, a raspberry flavoured jelly made with equal quantities of milk and water – and then whisked. It was like a beautiful pink tongue, dotted with spittle, and it tasted slippery. I had not been found out, had received no punishment, and life was getting back to normal again. I gargled with salt and water, on Sundays longed for visitors that never came, and on Monday mornings had all my books newly covered so that the teacher would praise me. Ever since the scandal she was enjoining us to go home in pairs, to speak Irish and not to walk with any sense of provocation.

Yet she herself stood by the fire grate, and after having hitched up her dress petted herself. When she lost her temper she threw chalk or implements at us, and used very bad language.

It was a wonderful year for lilac and the window sills used to be full of it, first the big moist bunches, with the lovely cool green leaves, and then a wilting display, and following that, the seeds in pools all over the sill and the purple itself much sadder and more dolorous than when first plucked off the trees.

When I daydreamed, which was often, it hinged on Eily. Did she have a friend, did her husband love her, was she homesick and above all was her body swelling up? She wrote to her mother every second week. Her mother used to come with her apron on, and the letter in one of those pockets, and sit on the back step and hesitate before reading it. She never came in, being too shy, but she would sit there while my mother fetched her a cup of raspberry cordial. We all had sweet tooths. The letters told next to nothing, only such things as that their chimney had caught fire, or a boy herding goats found an old coin in a field, or could her mother root out some old clothes from a trunk and send them to her as she hadn't got a stitch. 'Tis style enough she has' her mother would say bitterly, and then advise that it was better to cut my hair and not have me go around in ringlets, because as she said 'Fine feathers make fine birds.' Now and then she would cry and then feed the birds the crumbs of the biscuit or shortbread that my mother had given her.

She liked the birds and in secret in her own yard made little perches for them, and if you please hung bits of coloured rags, and the shaving mirror for them, to amuse themselves by. My mother had made a quilt for Eily and I believe that was the only wedding present she received. They parcelled it together. It was a red flannel quilt, lined with white and had a herringbone stitch around the edge. It was not like the big soft quilt that once occupied the entire window of the draper's, a pink satin onto which one's body could sink, then levitate. One day her mother looked right at me and said 'Has she passed any more worms?' I had passed a big tapeworm and that was a talking point for a week or so after the furore of the wedding had died down. Then she gave me half a crown. It was some way of thanking me for being a friend of Eily's. When her son was born the family received a wire. He was given the name of Jack, the same as his father and I thought how the witch had been right when she had seen the initial twice, but how we had misconstrued it and took it to be glad tidings.

Eily began to grow odd, began talking to herself, and then her lovely hair began to fall out in clumps. I would hear her mother tell my mother these things. The news came in snatches, first from a family who had gone up there to rent grazing, and then from a private nurse who had to give Eily pills and potions. Eily's own letters were disconnected and she asked about dead people or people she'd hardly known. Her mother meant to go by bus one day and stay overnight, but she postponed it until her arthritis got too bad and she was not able to go out at all.

Four year later, at Christmas time Eily, her husband and their three children paid a visit home and she kept eyeing everything and asking people to please stop staring at her, and then she went round the house and looked under the beds, for some male spy whom she believed to be there. She was dressed in brown and had brown fur-backed gloves. Her husband was very suave, had let his hair grow long, and during the tea kept pressing his knee against mine, and asking me which did I like best, sweet or savoury. The only moment of levity was when the three children, got in, clothes and all, to a pig trough and began to bask in it. Eily laughed her head off as they were being hosed down by her mother. Then they had to be put into the settle bed, alongside the sacks of flour, and the brooms, and the bric-à-brac, while their clothes were first washed and then put on a little wooden horse to dry before the fire. They were laughing but their teeth chattered. Eily didn't remember me very clearly and kept asking me if I was the eldest or the middle girl in the family. We heard later that her husband got promoted, and was running a little shop and had young girls working as his assistants.

I was pregnant, and walking up a street in a city, with my own mother, under not very happy circumstances, when we saw this wild creature coming towards us talking and debating to herself. Her hair was grey and frizzed, her costume was streelish, and she looked at us, and then peered, as if she were going to pounce on us, and then she started to laugh at us, or rather to sneer, and she stalked away and pounced on some other persons. My mother said 'I think that was Eily,' and warned me not to look back. We both walked on, in terror, and then ducked into the porch-way of a shop, so that we could follow her with our eyes, without ourselves being seen. She was being avoided by all sorts of people, and by now she was shouting something and brandishing her fist and struggling to get heard. I shook, as indeed the child within me was induced to shake, and for one moment I wanted to go down that street to her, but my mother held me back and said that she was dangerous, and that in my condition I must not go. I did not need much in the way of persuading. She moved on and by now several people were laughing, and looking after her and I was unable to move, and all the gladness of our summer day, and a little bottle of 'Mischief', pressed itself into the palm of my hand again, and I saw her lithe and beautiful as she once was, and in the street a great flood of light pillared itself around a little cock of hay that was dancing about, on its own.

I did go in search of her years later. My husband waited up at the cross, and I went down the narrow steep road with my son, who was thrilled to be approaching a shop. Eily was inside the counter, her head bent over a pile of bills that she was attaching to a skewer. She looked up and smiled. The same face but much coarser. Her hair was permed and a newly-pared pencil protruded from it. She was pleased to see me and at once reached out and handed my son a fistful of rainbow toffees.

It was the very same as if we'd parted only a little while ago. She didn't shake hands, or make any special fuss, she simply said 'Talk of an angel', because she had been thinking of me that very morning. Her children were helping, one was weighing sugar, the little girl was funnelling castor oil into four-ounce bottles, and her eldest son was up on a ladder fixing a flex to a ceiling light. He said my name, said it with a sauciness as soon as she introduced me, but she told him to whist. For her own children she had no time, because they were already grown but for my son she was full of welcome and kept saying he was a cute little fellow. She weighed him on the big meal scales, and then let him scoop the grain with a little trowel, and let it slide down the length of his arm and made him gurgle.

People kept coming in and out and she went on talking to me while still serving them. She was complete mistress of her surroundings and said what a pity that her husband was away, off on the lorry, doing the door-to-door orders. He had given up banking, found the business more profitable. She winked each time she hit the cash register, letting me see what an expert she was. Whenever there was a lull, I thought of saying something but my son's pranks commandeered the occasion. She was very keen to offer me something and ripped the glass paper off a two-pound box of chocolates and lay them before me, slantwise, propped against a can or something. They were eminently inviting, and when I refused she made some reference to the figure.

'You were always too generous,' I said sounding like my mother or some stiff relation.

'Go on,' she said and biffed me.

It seemed the right moment to broach it, but how?

'How are you,' I said. She said that as I could see she was topping, getting on a bit, and the children were great sorts and the next time I came I'd have to give her notice so that we could have a singsong. I didn't say that my husband was up at the road, and by now would be looking at his watch and saying 'Damn' and maybe would have got out to polish or do some cosseting to the vintage motor car, that he loved so. I said and again it was lamentable, 'Remember the old days Eily.'

'Not much,' she said.

'The good old days,' I said.

'They're all much of a muchness,' she said.

'Bad,' I said.

'No, busy,' she said. My first thought was that they must have drugged the feelings out of her, they must have given her strange brews and along with quelling her madness they had taken her spark away. There are times when the thing we are seeing changes before our very eyes, and if it is a landscape we praise nature, and if it is a spectre we shudder or cross ourselves but if it is a loved one that defects, we excuse ourselves and say we have to be somewhere, and are already late for our next appointment.

She kissed me and put a little holy water on my forehead, delving it in deeply, as if I were dough. They waved to us and my son could not return those waves encumbered as he was with the various presents that both the children and Eily had showered on him. It was beginning to spot with rain, and what with that and the holy water and the red rowan tree bright and instinct with life, I thought that ours indeed was a land of shame, a land of murder and a land of strange sacrificial women.

Over

Oh my dear I would like to be something else, any
thing else, an albatross. In short I wish I never knew
you. Or could forget. Or be a bone – you could suck it
Or a stone in the bottom of your pocket, slipped down
if you like, through one of the holes in the lining and
wedged into the hem more or less for ever, until you
threw the coat away or gave it to one of your relations
I never saw you in a coat only in a sort of jacket, what
they call an anorak. A funny word.

The first time you came to see me you were on the
point of leaving as I opened the door. Leaving already
Yes you were that intrepid. So was I. You asked me
where you might put your coat, or rather that anorak
thing and I couldn't think, there being no hall stand
Do you remember the room was too big for us. I remember. Seeing you sitting an ocean away, on a print-
covered chair, ill at ease, young, younger than your
thirty years and I thought how I would walk across
somehow or even stride across and cradle you. It was
too grand the room, the upright piano, the cut glass
chandelier. I have had notions of grandeur in the past
but they are vanishing. Oh my God, everything is
vanishing, except you.

A younger man. I go over our years ahead; jump
ahead if you will. I will be grey before you. What a
humbling thing. I will dye my tresses, all my tresses.

Perhaps I should experiment now with a bottle of brown dye and a little soft brush, experiment even with my hidden hairs. I must forestall you always, always. Leave no loopholes, nothing that will disappoint, or disenchant you. What nonsense, when you have already gone. I don't expect to see you again unless we bump into one another. I think I am getting disappointed in you and that is good. Excellent. You told me yourself how you lied to me. You are back from your lecturing and probably thinking of getting in touch with me, probably at this very moment. Your hand on the telephone, debating, all of you debating. Now you've taken your hand away. You've put it off. You know you can, you can put it aside like a treat, a childhood treat.

I did that as a child with a watch. Not a real watch but still a watch. It was the colour of jam, raspberry colour and I left it somewhere in fact in a vestibule in order that I could go and look at it, in order to see it there, mine, mine.

I did it. I crossed the room and what you did was to feel my hair over and over again and in different ways, touch it, with the palm of your hand, your drink was in your other hand (at first you refused a drink), felt it, strands of hair with your fingers, touched it as if it were cloth, the way a child touches its favourite surfaces such as a doll or a toy.

I keep saying child. It was like that, and you staring, staring, right through me, into me.

No knowing what I surrendered that night, what I gave up. I gave up most people, and gave up the taste for clothes and dinners and anything that could be called frivolous. I even gave up my desire to talk to intrude or make my presence felt. I went right back; that is true, right back to the fields, so to speak, where I grew up. All the features of that place, the simplest things, the sensations repossessed me. Crystal clear. A gate, a hasp, a water trough, the meadows and the way one can flop down into the corner of a field, a hay field. Dew again. And the image I had was of the wetness that babies and calves and foals have when they are just born and are about to be licked, and yet I was the mother.

Undoubtedly I was the mother when I gave you that soup and peeled a potato for you and cut it in half and mashed it as if you couldn't do it yourself and you said 'I have a poor appetite'. You thought I should have been more imposing. Even my kitchen you liked, the untidiness and the laurel leaves in a jug. They last a long time and I am told that they are lucky.

I should have enjoyed that night, that first un-planned meeting. As a matter of fact I did but it has been overlaid with so much else that it is like something crushed, something smothered, something at the bottom of a cupboard that has been forgotten, its very shape destroyed, its denomination ignored, and yet it is something that will always be there, except that no one will know or care about it, and no one will want to retrieve it and in the years to come if the cupboard should be cleaned out, if for instance, the occupants are leaving, it will indeed be found but it will be so crumpled as to be useless.

I dreamt of you before I met you. That was rash. I dream of you still, quite unedifying dreams where you are embracing me and whispering and we are inter-rupted the way we are constantly interrupted in life. You once told me that there was only ten minutes left for us because you had to buy a piece of perspex for a painting, make sure of getting it before the shops closed. The painting was a present to you both. It must have been in lieu of a wedding present.

Yes, I believe you are afraid of her. You say it's pity that holds you. But I believe that you are afraid of her and don't know it, and I believe that you love her and don't know it. You don't know very much about yourself, you shirk that. I asked you once, I went down on my knees, I asked you to go away for three days, without her or me or anyone and you looked at me as if I were sending you to Van Diemen's Land.

And another thing, you told me the same stories the same escapades. You seem to forget that you have already told me that story when you broke bottles of champagne, stole them and then broke them. In your youth. And how you pity chambermaids, make the bed with them, that is to say help them with the tuckings. Another virtue of yours is that you never flirt. You don't trade on your good looks and really you deserve a beautiful young girl. I don't think you are in your right mind. Neither am I. We should never have met. I do believe it's a tribal thing. When I saw your daughter I thought it was me. No, not quite. I thought, or rather I knew I was once her. She looked at me like a familiar. That gaze. She didn't make strange. I touched her all over. I had to touch her. I had to tickle her, her toes, her soft knees (like blancmange she was), her little crevices, and she smiled up at me and you said 'Smile for your auntie' and I was glad you called me Auntie, it was so ordinary and so plain and put me in the same circle as you.

Couldn't we all live together, couldn't we try. I used to be so jealous, green with it as they say, eaten up. I still am but couldn't we ride that way, the way the waves, the white horses, ride the sea. When I said it to you the mere suggestion made you panic, which makes me realize of course that you are not able for it, you are not up to it, you are only able for lies, you are only able for deceit.

So one day you will disappear for ever. Maybe you have. Isn't there some way of letting me know. I had so many wishes concerning us, but I had one in particular the smallest most harmless one and it was this: that one day I would come in from the outside and you would be here, already waiting for me, quite at home, maybe the kettle on or a drink poured. Not an outlandish wish. I suppose you wouldn't have wanted to make the journey without the certainty of seeing me. You said that coming up the street you always wondered what I would look like and what I would be wearing. I wear brown now. I suppose it's to be sombre.

After your baby smiled you put her on the swivel chair and I watched her and you watched me, and your friend whom you'd brought as a safety measure, was watching you watching me and the baby watched over us all. It was a perfect moment. I know that. None of us wanted it to end. Your friend knew. He knew how much I loved you and maybe he knew how much you loved me but neither you nor I knew it because we didn't dare to and possibly never will.

Possibly and perhaps – your two favourite words. Damn it. You see, I had just got used to the possibility of nobody, a barren life, when you came along. Of course you don't believe that, you think with all my frocks and my bracelets and my platform shoes that I am always gallivanting. The truth is I used to. I have collected those garments over the years and that parasol you saw was given to me once on my way to a bullfight. About a year ago – I stopped gallivanting. It is not that I want to be good, no. If anything I want to be bad because I would like it to end without its being too sickly. Endings are hideous. Take flowers for instance, some go putrid, the very sweetest smelling of all go putrid – so does parsley. I would like it just to shrivel away. It mustn't though.

The strangest thing is he lost his parents too at a young age. My father that is. You see, I am mixing you up with everyone, my father, my mother, my former husband, myself. Could you not come, could you not contact me now, so I could tell you about them, their customs and their ways. The whole parish I know. The lady called Josie walking out for three evenings with a man and saying 'I have no story to tell,' meaning was he going to propose to her, and next day he sent for a tray of engagement rings. He must have done it out of fright. Later she went mad. People depend on each other so much. Too much. You listen to me all right, in fact you repeat things that I say. My thoughts are like sprouts, like sprouts on the branch of your brain. Why are you so cold so silent. Your element is mercury.

All sorts of things remind me of you. On a dump today I saw a remains of a gas cooker and a Christmas tree though we're bang in the middle of the year. Christmas. That will rankle. You will celebrate it with your family as you did last year. Well anyhow it looked pathetic, out in the rain – a small gas oven and a Christmas tree with a stump of clay around it. I stood and looked at it. I had a feeling that you might come around the corner, swiftly the way you do. We would not have needed to say anything, you would have understood. That is the worse thing that at times you understand.

We were seen twice in public. I hated you buying me drinks but you refused to allow me to. I wanted to slip you a note but couldn't. As a matter of fact I lost all my confidence and quite a few of my movements. I was ashamed to remove my coat even though I was sweating. I thought it would make me seem too much at home and after all I had asked you there and you hadn't wanted to come, you had resisted even to the extent that you couldn't think of the name of a pub despite the fact that it was your district and what I had to do was go there and prowl around and find a quiet one and ring you. You allowed me to ring because she was away, staying with her sister. Her sister is an invalid. You seemed to imply that she had harmed herself. Are they a hysterical family, are they musical. Shall we call her Bimba. I can't use her name, that would be too friendly. I dream of her death, in her sleep, in an aeroplane crash. Anyhow in the pub you made me promise, take an oath, that I would never ring again. I took an oath. Is that commendable? I was thinking of you even as I sat there and promised, I was thinking of you, in another state altogether, a former state, a state of grace, a you saying 'I'll always come back to you, always, there's nothing else,' and I was thinking of the expression attached to that time, the sad eyes and so forth. Your eyes pierce people. You may say it again with your sad true eyes. Anything may happen, anything.

Anyhow, to get back to my father and yours. There are resemblances and there are differences. Yours loved his wife and died soon after her, to rejoin her in the next world. You felt left out maybe, excluded as a child. In the middle of a family, neither the youngest nor the eldest. My father's parents also died within a short space of one another. Pneumonia. Winter time and snow at the funeral and snow falling in on the coffin and then the four children divided up among cousins and the method of division was that each child was told to choose which pony and trap it wanted to be in, and in so doing choose its future home. Not a scrap of love had he. Once when he was sick he hid in the harness room and when he was found the woman of the house gave him a good thrashing and then a laxative. Not a scrap of love had he.

Maybe you're like him somewhere in the centre of you, maybe you're alike. No you're not. You're as un-alike as chalk and cheese. You have nature. He lacks it. Not many people have nature. And not many people have gentleness. Take my next-door neighbours, they shout and go around in dressing gowns, and as their friends arrive they shout even louder, and the hostess puts on a horrible red raincoat when she wants to go and get something from her car and it happens to be raining. I have a dreadful feeling that she's trying to impress me with her shouting and her car and her rain wear.

It's teeming today. Wouldn't you know. I have a feeling a very definite feeling that it might not cease, might turn into a second flood. We will all be incarcerated wherever we happen to be. Are you indoors, are you addressing a meeting, are you, or rather were you on your way to a bus stop and been obliged to take shelter under a tree. You said you had no knowledge of ever in your life missing anybody. Yes I think it might rain for ever or at least for forty days and forty nights. That is a form of ever. I will smash these chandeliers

51

bit by bit. It won't be difficult. They break easily, once when we were washing them a few of the pieces crumbled. The woman who was helping me couldn't understand why I laughed, neither could I.

She gave me a bit of advice, said by loving you I was closing the door to all other suitors.

Maybe you are in bed making love to her, or just caressing, the curtains drawn. Anyhow your rooms are so small that if you are indoors you are bound to be very close. I can see it, the little room, the sofa, the cushions, and, I never told you this but there are three ornaments in that room identical to three ornaments of mine. I shall not tell you now either as I am leaving you to guess.

If only we had been more exuberant. I went there three times in all, two of them against your will. The last time I was hungry as it happened. You offered me nothing. Are you by any chance a miserly man. I dearly wanted a keepsake of you and true enough on one of these unfortunate visits you gave me a handkerchief to dry my eyes, but it was a new one and had nothing of your person on it. I cried a lot. I wonder who washed it. You wash your own trousers because when I inquired about the white round stains on them you said it was where you had spattered on the undiluted bleach. I could have told you. I wish I had them. If I could hold them now – would hold them and hug them and press them to me.

It is not right to love so. I suppose there is a sickness of heart as well as a sickness of mind and body. Yes when you first came I really had reached a point where I had stopped looking and you appeared at my door with a pamphlet and you were leaving again and I liked the look of you and I invited you in. They call it fate. I still see your face in the window pane, appearing, disappearing, reappearing. Oh my God, a face.

Don't get married, or if you do, tell me, give me warning so that I can get used to it. I won't give you a wedding present. What an ugly thing to say. Yes it's ugly. This house is upside down, that drawing-room that you saw, well, it's a shambles and there are glasses lying around and the plants haven't been watered, or if they have it has been reckless, too much water one day so that they brimmed over, then none for days. There are little pools of water on the floor and those that have dried up have left white marks upon the parquet not unlike the bleach on your trousers. How long is it now. My God it is all a matter of how long it is. The days are jumbled. Just now, lying on my bed – another fatal habit – I saw the tree that I always see, the plane tree, its leaves, and would you believe it it seemed to me that the bits of sky that I saw through the leaves were leaves also, different-coloured leaves, serrated at the edges, so I saw tree leaves and cloud leaves. I am losing my reason. The garden is soggy, a wreck. And although it is summer I definitely smell autumn. I keep thinking that by autumn it will have improved a bit. Then again I think that you will have come back as you threatened to, and that we will be together in the darkest light, under covers, talking, touching the most terrible reconciliations uttered, uttering. Do you know that in your sleep I stroke and stroke you and when you waken, no matter how late the hour you always say 'A lovely way to waken' and you always stayed a few minutes longer, defied time, and yes, come to think of it those were our most valuable moments. You were at your best then and without fear. I stood at the door to see you off and only once did you look back. I expect you hate farewells.

The last fling I had was not like this at all, except that he was actually hitched, married. An odd fellow. A Harry. We spent five days away from his country and mine, though in a country much similar, dark and craggy and with a heavy rainfall. Some interesting excavations there, skeletons intact in peat. We drove a lot. He told me how he loved his wife, always did, always would. Wives do not come out too badly in the human maul. We had the same thing each day for lunch – salt bread, and herrings and a small glass of spirit. When we got to our destination we had a suite and one set of windows faced the sea and another set faced the dormitory town. We picked stones the first morning. I found a beautiful white stone, nearly pearl. I wanted to give it to you. I gave it to a friend of yours, a man you brought here. I didn't do it to make you jealous but rather to let you know that if all this weight didn't exist between us I would be able to be nice to you and maybe you in your turn would be nice to me and even funny and even frivolous. Yes we once made the noise of turkeys, beeping.

As I got to know this man Harry, he decreased in my estimation. He made a point of telling me about other loves of his and there was always a lot of blood in question. One story of his concerned a very beautiful Spanish virgin, all about her beauty and her moisture, etc. On the very last evening just as he was consulting the menu for dinner he said he hoped I had money because he hadn't brought very much. You see I was ashamed of him and that is why I paid. Whereas when we went to an hotel, you, who could scarcely afford it, paid. And you set the clock twenty minutes before we were due to waken up so that we could be together for one of those lovely moments those lovely series of moments. Even you who profess to miss nothing, can you tell me you don't miss those. That morning in the hotel was when you first talked of love and made a plan for the future, our future. That morning you lost your head. You must have imagined yourself as someone else or that you could have explained it all to her, ironed it all out. You were quite practical. You said it would take five weeks, but instead of that you were back in a week and I might have known something was amiss because you came early and you drank heavily and you said could we talk could we talk. We talked. You said you had rows with her, two dirty rows and then at the very end you said you collapsed into one another.

Sweet Jesus never have I known such a stab. That collapse, I could actually see it and feel it. I saw the hour, it was dawn and your tiredness and hers and both of you washed out and one or other of you saying – it matters not which of you – saying 'What am I saying, what am I doing' and then the collapse, lying down, in your clothes, fitting in a bit of sleep until your baby stirred, and one of you went to tend to it while the other prepared two cups of tea. Maybe while you were shaving you called in and said 'hey, I hope I didn't give you a black eye'. Of course it was not all erased, nor indeed forgotten, but it was over, it was behind you and you had accomplished something, shown your ugly colours and got nearer to one another.

I brought you nearer, God help us. Most probably you went out for the day maybe you went to the library. But no doubt you said roughly what time you would be back and that is the thing. You made it known that you would be back whatever the hour. That was the second bitterest thing for there is another.

The evening – one of the three occasions when I telephoned and dropped the phone out of shock and then re-dialled and later saw you in the pub – I asked if I could have a child of yours. You told me point blank that it was impossible, also you inferred that I was too old, what with my divorce and my children reared and all that. Then after a few whiskies you decided to invite me back to your house and on the way back you allowed me to link you until we got near your street and then you ran on ahead so as not to be spied upon and I followed slightly ashamed, and as I said, like a dog.

Still inside the house you were different. The moment you discovered that your baby hadn't smothered itself or wasn't kidnapped or wasn't choking you kissed me fondly, fond kisses, many of them, and you removed my coat, and later as we fell talking you said that in the morning you had got someone to mind your child and you had gone to market and brought razor blades and white cotton handkerchiefs, one of which you offered me – and then came the second and bitterest blow, because as you were telling me I realized that you had had free time, that you could have seen me that you could have contacted me that for once you were not tied to her but you didn't and I realized that it wasn't she who always came between us. Sometimes it was you.

Guessing my thoughts you said you loved no one and were only interested in your educational work. When you remember that night, that is if ever you let loose the hogs of memory, if they stalk, do you remember the subsequent time, the goat skin, you, me, us, perfect then. You can't have forgotten it all. Couldn't you have written. Ah yes you did. A circumspect little letter about how you mustn't get out of your depth how it mustn't be allowed to blossom. Well it didn't. Yes it did. It blossomed and what's more it caught fire, a whole forest of fire.

And another thing you have softened me towards others. I am prepared to nurse my aged father and my aged mother when the time comes and they call on me. Shall I tell you why. I think by your expression and by one or two things that you say that you did want to be by my side, and constantly, but that a sense of duty restrained you and a comparison. I needed you less than her. It seems to you that I have advantages over her. Which reminds me I haven't told you about the boy who died. I feel responsible, no not responsible but somehow involved.

The day I met you I also met another good-looking young man, a doctor in fact. He was a new doctor that I had gone to and he took a bit of a shine to me. I'd gone about my depression. A thing I didn't want you to know. He saw how it was and he prescribed accordingly. Later that day I met you having taken the first set of tablets and already believing that magic was at work.

The young doctor visited me in a private capacity that is after I had met you. He kissed me, yes. By then I was so enraptured with you that I was nice to everybody. I let him kiss me. I remember our exact conversation, his describing a Caesarian birth, putting his two hands in and lifting the imaginary baby out. He said Caesarian babies had less gumption because they didn't have to push. He was telling me all this and I was remarking to myself how deftly his nostrils flared in and out and then he went a bit far demonstrating this Caesarian to me and I jumped off the cushions. That was another thing. He arranged the cushions for us to loll on. You never did that. You sat at a distance. We talked stiffly. After a long time and nearly always as you were about to leave you asked if you might come and kiss me and quite often we met halfway across the room like two animals, little animals charging into one another. Only once did you rebuff me altogether, you said did I have to be so demonstrative. I rushed towards you and embraced you and you threw me off. You even said that if we did make love it would preclude its ever happening again.

Why did you say that? To punish me for going to your house for pleading with you. And on the way out I said 'Are you angry' and you said no but that maybe I was, a little. Of course I was. Not a little, a lot. Another time you said did I have to talk so much. The trouble is I talked to no one else in between. That is the worst of putting all one's eggs in one basket. I loved your smell. You may have heard it from others but you smell of gardens, not flower gardens but herb gardens and grasses and plants and dock and all those rampant things.

Do you use the same words exactly, and exactly the same caresses, the same touch, the same hesitation, the same fingering. Are you as shy with her as with me. If only you had had courage and a braver heart.

I do believe we would have been happy. It is perhaps foolish to say so but there was nothing in you that I did not like and admire. Even your faults even your forgetfulness. There was nothing in you that clashed with me. You were startled once by the flowers very white flowers they were with very thick blossom. You admired them. It was as if you had never seen flowers before, or certainly never seen those. You made me feel as if I had cultivated them as if they were an extension of me.

I heard from that friend you brought that she is more demanding, makes her needs felt. You found a lack in me. You told me I am kind. I did a favour for your friend but that was only to woo you.

I am not kind, I cut people off as with the shears and I drop them, like nettles. At this moment there are several people who could do with my company and I withhold it and that poor cat sits day after day on the window ledge or outside the door and when I open it to take in the milk that poor black cat tries to slink in but I kick it with my shoe, in fact with the heel of my shoe. The same black cat as I held on my breast one night when you came and I was lounging. That was a false moment but I had to vary things because the previous time you said it was unnatural to spend so many hours over a dinner table and I felt that already it was all getting a bit stale, and I wished in my heart that you would invent something, that you would think up some new plan, some diversion, arrange for us to meet elsewhere. Of course you couldn't. There was a matter of secrecy and shortage of money. When I am short of money I borrow and to tell you the truth my debts are catching up with me, but when you are short you go without. I wanted to give a big cushion to your child. You refused. At the same time as you swore me to secrecy I broke that pledge. I told a few of my women friends and then you introduced me to a few of your men friends. I think you were showing me off. Come to think of it we were like children. It is just as well it got nowhere.

Yes there are times when I think the whole thing seems ridiculous. For instance the night you were to come to dinner or rather one of the nights you were to come to dinner and after waiting for about two hours I got restless and began to walk back and forth, paced, and did little things hoping that would speed you up – changed my shoes, brushed my hair, thumped the piano, kept opening and shutting the door. It was winter then and I could tell the seconds passing by a lot of ways but most of all by the candle burning down. It was a blue candle. At length I couldn't bear it any longer so I turned down the stove – I always had food that could be kept hot – and went out without a coat to wait at the bus stop. And do you know something, there was a moment standing there, an absolute moment when I mistook someone else for you. Yes I was convinced. I saw him at the top of the bus, wild hair, the anorak and then I saw him rise and I saw his back as he went down the stairs of the bus and I got myself ready to smile, to kiss, to reach out my hand, and yes I was shaking and excited as if it were you.

I wish it had been. That was the second occasion I went to your house. A very cold reception. You kept on the television. I was prepared to end it and the next day you appeared out of breath and you sat and you talked and you said how it would all improve and everything would be better between us.

Did you believe that then? I must confess I did. That particular evening, the objects – the room getting dark, the end of the blue candle, the two of us thinking that the worst of our troubles were behind us.

You had to go away next day. Away. Of course there are ruses for passing the time. I didn't see my friends, alas I have abandoned my friends but what I did do was to go to cafés where it was very full and very noisy. I searched them out but no matter how full a café is, there is always room for one, usually at someone else's table. The way they argued or looked into one another's eyes. I was having a rest from you. I could tell the lesbians even though they couldn't tell and those who would be together for ever and those who wouldn't. I had such a way of seeing into them, such clarity. That is another thing. I often see you as an old man and you are in a trench-coat, white with the belt hanging down, one of those stiff trench-coats, with perforations under the arm, and you are recuperating from some illness and you are, yes, a disillusioned man. It will all be behind you then, she and I, and your daughter and your life's work, and how will you remember it, how?

In those restaurants they play waltzes. I loved the first bars of the waltz. I often stood up to dance, with my mind meandering. Yes that has been my life of late, restaurants, people saying to each other, 'Happy?', and people saying what François said and how much of that hair they should cut.

I did something awful. Friends of mine were going away on a boat for ever, and I didn't see them off. It was my godson going away for ever and I didn't see him off. I thought you might have been ringing and I didn't want to be out.

My lovely godson. I sent him a cup and saucer to the cabin but it is not the same thing. You see I had a moment with him, unique, I think it was tantamount to a sexual moment. It was this.

I had been in his house once, or rather in their garden and there was a party in full swing. A lot of people, a lot of drinking and jabber, and he and I sat far apart from the others, under a tree, asking riddles. There were flies bothering us and we used to blow them away and he told me about his dreams when he was always winning and then he said would I like to walk around, to go out of the garden. And we did that, we went out and walked all around the clapboard fence, and met a lady, a sort of serving lady going in with a platter of strawberries, and he held my hand and squeezed it on and off, and when we got back to our starting point and were just about to go in by the lych gate he pointed to the nearby woods and told me there was a dirty man in there who pulled down his trousers and showed his butt and then we hurried in. I didn't see him off.

And another thing, I bought fire irons – don't ask me why, because it's summer – and I tried to beat the lady down about the price. I went to her private house having got the address from the assistant and when she opened the door I saw that I was confronted by a hunchback and still I tried to beat her down about the price. It was nothing. A matter of shillings. I stood there waiting for her to concede and she did. We are to be pitied.

Another haunt of mine is cinemas, before they open. Oh my God, they have to be seen to be believed. Shabby. Quite a long way from Strauss and the waltzes. Usherettes, mostly elderly ladies and people like myself, killing time in the afternoon. I want all my teeth drawn out of me and other teeth, molars, if you will, stuck back into my gums. I want to grind these new teeth, these molars to a pulp. Perhaps I want to eat you alive. Ah yes the seat of this love must indeed be a hate. So the smart alecs would tell me. The hate extends to others. Good friends. How boring they have become. They tell me the shape of their new rooms, or the colours of their walls and what they eat in restaurants. Most terrible bilge. I get listless. Then I get angry. I have to leave right in the middle of their conversations. Mostly I don't see them.

I don't work now. Waiting. It gets on one's nerves. I can keep going a little longer but only a little. One good thing about being out is that I imagine you telephoning. I exist on that little ploy for hours. I even live your disappointment with you. Your phoning once, then again immediately then asking the operator to get the number, then phoning again in about an hour and another hour, and concluding that I have gone somewhere, abroad maybe as far as Morocco, when all the time I am in one of those cafés listening to one of those waltzes, thinking of you or in one of those cinemas waiting for the performance to start, reading a sign that says 'Fruits and ices', unable to stop thinking of you. It can't be hate. Do you ever imagine me with another man. You offered me one of your friends once, the night we were all together, here, dancing and cavorting and laughing. Laughing we were. 'Why don't you have Mike' you said. But your arms were all around me and anyhow we were on the landing, on our way to bed. Believe me, I even wanted you to feed and drink off me. I wanted to waste away in your service. To be a bone.

Am I saying wanted when I actually mean want? It is still my purpose, still my intention. You forbade me the gift of having your child and I was too honest or else too cowardly to betray you, to dupe you. Maybe

you have taken the plunge, maybe you have go
married and that is why you are not showing yourself
You told me once that you muttered something abou
it. You mutterer. That doctor I mentioned got killed
in a plane crash along with a hundred others. You may
get killed. Do you know what I hate about myself, I
have never done a brave thing, I have never risked
death. If only I had done something you could have
admired me by. If only I'd renounced you. She is by
your side. Your guardian angel, perhaps your little
help mate? Not from what I know of her. You told me
little but you inferred a lot. We are so hard on our
selves. Ah yes, those waltzes in those restaurants make
me cry, and so do mushrooms. If only I could hear your
voice for a minute, half a minute, less. You go from
place to place. She is by your side, whether you like it
or not. I often imagine you in trains sitting opposite
each other saying the odd word, then getting off, the
two of you sharing the carrier cot. What bliss.

Tell me, is she pretty, is she soft, your lady, or does
she have what is called a whim of iron? I did ask you
once if she had blue eyes and you professed not to
know. You must know. It is not that I am a lover of
blue eyes, the question simply cropped up. You must
have seen them in all lights, and at all moments, maybe even in childbirth. On these numerous train journeys, do you ever think of me? I know you do. I am
certain of it. I can feel you thinking of me even now.
You may carry the thought through. You may contact
me. Yes he died, that young doctor. I am glad that I
didn't make love to him. I would not care to have made
love to a dead man. Yes it got killed between us, you
and I. Contravened. That is a fact, a bitter fact. It
wasn't that it didn't happen, oh it did. Oh how it hap-

pened. Your face and mine, your voice and mine. Evening. Just like milking time, and the cows lowing as if we were in the byre. Then the moon came up. Our faces shone. I could have touched the stars. One should be thankful for a moment, even grateful, and not be plaintive like this. Yes, it is nothing short of a miracle, the way you met me, more than halfway. The way you came out of your innerness and complexity and came to me, and I told you things, nonsense things. I told you for instance about the one wooden sweet, which was mixed up with all the other sweets in a carnival assortment. This wooden sweet had bright wrapping like all the others, and more than once I got it and I didn't know whether to be glad or sorry, and neither of us could tell why it was in the box in the first place, whether it was some sort of joke or the like. And you told me about having to undress at the doctors and having a dirty vest on, and being scolded by your mother. She was ashamed.

It is when I think about you suffering that I cannot bear it. I think of you crying. You cried lest you could never see me again and I said you always could and that I would always understand and be womanly and be patient. King Lear says women must be kind, or something to that effect. Yes that is what I must be, kind and womanly. I know what I will do. I will talk to your friend, Mike, the friend you brought here. I will tell him some little pleasantry and he will pass it on to you, and you will be touched, regaled. I will do that now.

Oh God, I have done it. I rang. He told me. You have gone away to a new country, a young country at that. Gone with your family. I knew it. It seems she

65

did something silly like her sister, something extreme. Oh how mad I was to think that she would give you up, that we would all share. Oh how cracked one's thoughts get. You did the right thing, the only thing. Yes, I will see you when you are old, just as I visualized it, in the off-white mackintosh with the perforations under the armpit and you will be convalescing. I suppose you're married. And yes, you have no nature. Oh God, send me some word, some sign, some token. Tell me if you are married, or if you've forgotten, tell me how you are. It has all been for nothing, tell me something, I have to know ... I will never know, I do not want to know now.

The Favourite

She was the third child and in all sorts of ways lucky. For one thing, she was born on the Sabbath day, and consequently was reputed to be fair and wise and good and gay. They were able to tell her in later life that she was a model little baby, had no faults, had contracted no fevers, except such harmless things as measles and mumps.

The first time she went to be vaccinated the doctor was over at the cross roads, delivering a baby from a tinker woman in her late fifties; and the second time the doctor was inebriated, sitting in his basket chair saying things were bad, odious bad, because he had just been disappointed in a promotion that he was expecting. Instead he gave her a little gift, an egg under green wire mesh, which when squeezed revealed a small canary-coloured chick. She played and played with it. She kept it at night in a nest made of chaff from the bottom layer of a box of chocolates. When they gave her turpentine for the tapeworms it was not like medicine at all but on a loaf of sugar, almost a treat, and having sucked the ugly taste away she used to let the little cube dissolve in her mouth, and savour it, slowly, slowly. The first day she was put on a bicycle, she managed to stay up, to steer it down the length of the flag, and around the corner, and only then did she jump off, and let the bicycle tumble into the privet hedge, but by then they were clapping and saying bravo bravo.

At school she did not distinguish herself, was not overbrainy like her elder sister, or fanciful like her younger sister, always came in the middle a few marks above a pass. But at the cookery class she shone, would be given charge of the fire, so that she was the first to taste a little of the boxty, or a little of the bubbling jam from the tart, or some of the steamed pudding or whatever. She had a pink bicycle, named after a witch, by the time she was ten, and soon after a blue basket for it, and later a crocheted cover for the saddle. People gave her things – her father gave her a foal so that she had a little investment while still in her puberty. If a neighbour wanted eggs, or cooking apples or pears for bottling, they would ask her, rather than one of her sisters, and she would convey the message to her mother and deliver these things, and receive a little money or a little gift as a reward. Then she never went out without bringing something back, a small packet of biscuits, two or three mushrooms, an item of news, something. Her pet name was Whitey, because of her blonde hair, and whenever her father came in from the fields and while he would still be taking off his boots he would say 'Where's Whitey?' and then upon seeing her, because she often hid behind the scullery door, sheltering behind an old trench-coat, or ducked down behind one of the sacks of flour, he would spot her and say 'There's my girl'; and oftener than not tell her how her foal was doing. Her rosary beads, white mother of pearl, had been blessed at Lourdes, and she had a special little filigree box to hold them in. Watching her pray in chapel, watching the beads slip slowly through her fingers, the dressmaker noted that they were a perfect match and a complement to her pearled teeth. If an umbrella happened to turn inside out Tess knew exactly what to do to get it right again and her mother had no qualms about lending her the one brown umbrella with the Lalique handle.

The day she went away to school everyone cried, her mother broke down, and quoting from a prayer, said life truly was a vale of tears. She had oodles of presents – silk hankies, georgette hankies, lawn hankies, hankie satchets, bottles of perfume, perfume sprays, scented stationery – more than she could fit. She hid them, or rather she placed them in the wooden cupboard where her summer clothes and her various toilet articles were neatly placed and no one was allowed to touch them until she came back for her hols. Soon the cupboard developed a beautiful smell from stationery, the opened tin of talc, and the perfume spray into which a drop of hair oil had been put in order to try its puffing powers. Her autograph book was there too and was full of loving inscriptions to her and promises of friendship for life. Except for the one wicked inscription –

> 'Thirty-two degrees is freezing point,
> What's squeezing point?'   Anon.

The convent was forty miles from home, in the western part of Connaught, and there was no bus service to it. She excelled herself there, was diligent, devout, the last to leave the chapel, and in no time at all tipped by the elder girls as a future prefect. No dandruff on the collar of her coat, no monkeying about with nail varnish, no muck on her shoes. After their daily walk she made a point of using the foot scraper, and as the head nun said was an example to all the Bolshies. She was one of the few girls who when she tied her hair back with a velvet ribbon was not asked to remove it nor did she have it confiscated. She had two best friends who vied agonizingly for her love, and then two or three stooges – youngsters whom she took under her wing and who did things for her – shone her shoes, dressed her bed, put a fresh supply of water in the ewer every evening, and left little love letters under her pillow. The two girls who loved her could not do enough for her, and there wasn't a day that she didn't receive an illicit bar of chocolate or a slice of cake, and to her delight the skeleton of a leaf, which was like a beautiful gauze brooch, and which she cherished.

During the Christmas holidays, togged out as she was, in a new blue suit and blue suède court shoes, she acquired her first boy-friend, an owner of a drapery shop, a dark-haired handsome athlete, and a great catch. In fact she stole him from a namesake of hers, at a dance and as a result she got called 'Pinch me'. She no longer liked the name Whitey – it was babyish. She wore her hair in very tight curls, millions of curls, and with her court shoes, wore nutmeg-coloured stockings.

His gift to her was a pair of fur-backed gauntlet gloves, and they arrived by post in a very long box that looked as if it might have contained a big fish. The family grouped around while she opened the parcel and then the exclamations were myriad. Along with being fur backed they were lined with fur, of grey and white squirrel, fur that was soft as a little puppy – while the gloves themselves were long and sleek and were laid out on the tissue paper for all to see, but none to touch. The workman marvelled at them and won-

dered what their raw materials were, what animals.
She wore them when she went for her evening fashion
parade. She set out for her walk always while it was
still light, because in that way she was able to elicit the
admiration of friends and neighbours. The routine
was, that she visited various houses, was treated to tea
and cake, then later to ciderette, and so numerous were
the calls she had to make, that often she would not get
back till midnight and then would have to be escorted
by one or other of the ladies of the house. On those
midnight walks their accents grew very grand and
their plans very lyrical as they discussed men and trous-
seaux and holidays abroad. There was a certain gloom
at home during her absence, and the moment they
heard the latch being lifted the family jumped up, and
were jostling each other to greet her and to hear the
news. She was the first to tell them of the plans for a
new cinema-cum-dance-hall, and of a rumour that the
doctor was going blind, and had seen stars in the dis-
pensary, earth stars as opposed to sky stars. When her
romance ended – the athlete went back to his former
love – she thought of returning the gloves, but decided
against it, and realized anyhow that he had gone back
to the other girl simply because he had been threatened
with a breach of promise. Asked about it she used to
say 'Poor Tom' and no more, so that she could not even
be accused of having a sharp tongue.

On her eighteenth birthday she received a beautiful
ring from her mother. The base was white gold, the
mount a black enamel paste with a little diamond in
the centre. It had been her mother's single treasure, an
heirloom, that had been removed solemnly from the
dead finger of a deceased aunt in Chicago. She was said

to resemble this aunt, in her beauty, in her gaiety, what with her high cheekbones, her blonde tresses and her gauntness. The aunt had in fact taken strychnine, and had poisoned herself, because of a broken heart, the result of a wronged love affair with a Swede. Whenever strychnine was brought into the house they would look at it, mesmerized by its blue-white flakiness, thinking of their aunt, its potency and the mystery of her being dead. But her sisters were much more intrigued by such morbidities than she was.

After the spell in the convent Tess went directly to the City of Dublin and commenced on a secretarial course. She lived in a hostel at first, loved taking walks at night, going window shopping, loved the new machine she was learning to type on, and was told by the teacher that she would have made a good pianist. Soon she passed the necessary examinations, applied for various posts, and became secretary to a most important man in a computer company. With her first wages she bought a table cloth for her mother and sent it by registered post. Her bicycle was sent to her by train, and in the office where she worked, the other girls used to beg her to let them take a spin around the enclosure at their lunch break. There was a pool of girls, about thirty in all, and then some men who held slightly higher positions.

Tess was the darling of them all. In the summer months they would fetch her bunches of roses, or bunches of lilac, or bunches of Canterbury bells, and very often a little punnet of strawberries or currants from their gardens. Many of them lived on the outskirts of the city and along with being given treats, Tess used to be invited out on Sundays.

She would go to Dollymount and walk barefoot over

the silver sands and see the sea in all its splendour, she would go to Howth Head, and see the sea from an opposite direction, and count the buoys in the ocean. She would go to Killiney and be told that it was a Little Naples. She would go out as far as Glendalough and hear the story of St Kevin tempted as he was by a voluptuous woman, and hear of his restraint. She would partake of boiled mutton for lunch, queen cakes for tea, and late on Sunday evenings she would be found coming home on the last train, her body jogging with it, tired but contented like most of the other passengers.

It was on one of these journeys that she met Luke, and the very approach was like everything else that fitted into the tapestry of her charmed life. He was a commentator an another train – an especially exciting train, comprising a journey in which visitors were told about the beauty spots, the historical significance of places, and the numerous legends attached to each hill and each dale. He listened to her talk to an old woman who was sitting opposite. The talk centred on begonias, because the woman was carrying a small bunch of them and they were a very dark arresting shade of red. They were as deep as if made of some sumptuous cloth. When the woman alighted and he closed the door, he asked more politely if he could have a word with Tess. Could he make a recording of her voice since it was like a lark, and would be a wonderful speciality on his train entertainment. As a reward she would be given a day trip to Killarney, be treated to a four-course lunch on board, and be able to see those famous lakes and the granite mountains. He walked her home to her digs, stood outside with her under the big linden tree and said the usual charming things, how that she was sparkling, that she was a rose, that together they would

73

go to Howth Head, together they would go to Dollymount, and run over the sands, together at night they
would go on that corkscrew road and look down at all
the little twinkling lights that constituted the enviable
residences of Little Naples. He got to know the things
she liked – coconut creams, ham paste and gin and lime.
He would devise little picnics for her, bringing small
jars of paste, biscuits sandwiched together, and the gin
and lime in a washed-out blue magnesia bottle. When
it transpired that he was a married man, she ended it
as neatly as it had begun, and the only sign that her
flatmates saw was that she took no supper and spent one
whole day and one whole night in bed, eyes shut but
not asleep. Her younger sister who shared the bed with
her kept wanting to say consoling things, but was afraid
to intrude, and the following morning when Tess was
dressing herself she announced that from then on, she
intended to go without sugar and sweet things.

When she met the young country excise officer she
saw at once that they were made for one another. They
exchanged a few remarks about songs, their hobbies
and the parts of Dublin they liked best. Her father
was raging. He forbade it. He kicked her in the backside and told her he would not hear of it. Her father
said there wasn't a man in the thirty-two counties of
Ireland worthy of her and she said 'Yes, Dad,' but still
went off in the evenings to meet the man with the curly
black hair. She used to wait at the entrance to the pitch
where he and the lads played football. Afterwards he'd
walk towards her and they'd link and go off, ap-
parently mindless of the whistles and insinuations that
were thrown at them. They were in complete contrast,
with her blonde hair and his black, and they walked as

if they were on air. As time went by, her father was asking the young man for tips for the horses, then for secret information as to the amount people received for their pensions, and then a request if perhaps the Government could be cajoled into giving him a loan to buy fertilizer for his land. The young man did everything he could to help and was really installed into the family, when he helped to save hay, in all his spare hours.

They were engaged within a month, and Tess changed the black enamel ring to the third finger of her right hand. Her engagement ring was a blue sapphire and there was much conjecture about its price.

For the wedding she had a bouquet of lily of the valley, plus a matching cloth tiara, and a dress made of baby blue tulle. At the breakfast afterwards, during the well-wishing speeches you could hear a pin drop, so awed were the guests. Her former boss said her name may be Tess but his name for her was Sunshine, her uncle spoke of a little present she had given him while still impecunious and a tot – a brown scapular, which he pulled out from behind his striped shirt, and dangled for all to see. Her father said she was one of the more favourite members of the family, causing her sisters to snigger, because she was in fact *the* favourite. She owned two yearlings and her younger sister thought it would be funny if they stalked into the big room, galloping like mad, and made havoc of the dishes and the cut glasses and the big three-tiered cake on its ridiculous frilled stand. Tess herself made a little speech and from the far end of the table a young man began to hum Lili Marlene. As she had always predicted her going-away suit was a saxe blue – box jacket and pleated skirt, with a very pale blue blouse that could be tied at the neck with a soft knot. Two of the waitresses who had got very drunk and had fallen under the table caught her by the ankle as she went by and mourned over her approaching vanquishment. Tess laughed it off.

Two of her four births were quite difficult but her husband was nearby, to hold her hand, his cousin, a doctor, did the delivery, the nurses were all pie, and Tess was congratulated upon her real courage. She did not care for breast feeding and her husband fully understood. They had a nurse for the babies, and built on an extra little wing to their house so that the nursery life could be in one place and the grown-up life in another. As well as his earnings, her husband had an income from his family, who owned a big sawmill and were said to be rolling in money. He was ever-generous and Tess used to say they'd die paupers.

In the evening when all his work was done, and his bit of gardening completed, he would stretch in front of the fire, give her a beck, say 'Come here' and put her sitting on his lap. Then they would admire the wall-paper, or the coal scuttle, or one of the many precious items in the china cabinet, that had been wedding presents to her. Eventually he would coax her to get up and make him a sandwich. Her sandwiches were wonderful. If people called unexpectedly she would always disappear into the kitchen and come back with a salver of them. She said it must have been something in her hands, because all she did was use up any bit of cold meat, add a pinch of salt, and a tomato or something to moisten it all, and 'Bob's your uncle.' But she was proud of it, and proud that so many people called,

especially new people who had come to take up temporary jobs – doctors, priests, bank clerks, school teachers.

Theirs was an old Georgian house at the top of the
market town and it was called The Shutters because
the previous owners had had jalousies put in. It was a
big Georgian house, but they got it reasonably because
the owners, two spinsters, had taken a shine to her husband and used to tease each other over him, and write
him little billets doux. Then Tess had gone to auc-
tions, and was crafty at bidding and getting bargains,
so that all the rooms were soon filled with heavy dark
brown mahogany pieces and with overmantels and
ornaments and jugs for artificial flowers. The spinsters
had sent to France for all the bedroom wallpaper and
so it happened that each bedroom seemed prettier than
the next. The house faced south so they got the best
aspect of the sun, and likewise the garden was a model
of construction and tillage. Flowers, fruits and vege-
tables grew side by side, the back wall had a series of
pear trees grafted along it, so that from her kitchen
window as she was peeling or chopping or ironing, Tess
could see the blossom, then the fruits forming, then the
big dun pears with irregular holes in them where the
wasps had been scooping the flesh out. She had a maid
to help her and a big tall boy, a bit soft in the head, to
dig in the garden. They had loganberries, raspberries,
various currant bushes, they made jam in the season
and bottled fruits in the autumn. Her parents came by
hired car the first Sunday of every month, and when
asked, Tess could honestly say 'Can't complain' about
any aspect of life.

They threw card parties, for the men, at Christmas,
and though she never played Tess went from table to

table – they fitted up little card tables – looking at the players' hands and making obscure but meaningful remarks such as 'Not bad Nicko' or 'That'll shake 'em'. Then at midnight, she served supper, cold meats, stuffing, sausage rolls, along with pots of tea so as to liven them up. Her father would sing the made-up song about the previous doctor, old and blind, who so loved the cards that he put up his own Arab pony and lost, and had to drag the trap home by the shafts, where his complaining wife, Dilly, met him at the top of the drive. The song brought to mind the old days and all the various card games – the tense situations where men at the very last minute made or lost their all, where tables were turned upside down because of treachery. Tess would then pass tumblers of hot punch around, and in no time, they would be clearing the dishes from the arbutus table, in order to start again. Her children would come in, in their pyjamas, to say good night, and sometimes would sing a hymn, usually Silent Night, and might be asked by one of the men if Santa Claus was up the chimney. Then she would dismiss them, stoke up the fire, and sit happily surrounded by all the obstreperous men. One of the younger players might say to her husband what a lucky man he was, and Tess would smile, smile, while not appearing to hear. The prizes were white turkeys, which would be hanging by their feet in the pantry, white and fluffy and unblemished except for the spot of blood around the throat, where their necks had been wrung, joyously wrung by the idiot. One year her husband won, Tess did the sporting thing – she raffled all the names, but omitted his.

The card games, the Bishop's visit, and whenever

their Mammy went away to have a new baby, constituted the epochs of the children's lives. They were wild
as hares, got lost for hours on end, fell off their bicycles
or were off up the country watching a cow calve, or a
cat having kittens. They would bring home rabbits or
kittens in cardboard boxes, and make pets of them, and
paint them, and put bows in their hair, and eventually
those self-same kittens would have to be drowned or
put in a sack and left in the middle of nowhere. Tess
was not an animal lover. All dogs, and they were all
mongrels, were called Biddy regardless of their sex,
and invariably died, of the same thing which was a
distemper. There were never less than six or seven at
table, sometimes a visiting child, and then again one
of theirs would be missing or on vacation. Tess had the
habit of calling them by the wrong names, as if all their
names were in her head jumbled together and it did
not matter too much which was which. She always took
an afternoon nap, and then the children would have to
go on tip-toe, or go down the garden, or play out in the
street, and someone, her favourite son, would be appointed to wake her at four.

He wrote poems for her, and left them on her dressing bureau and she would show them to her visitors
and say weren't they 'arch'. She preferred her sons. She
was rarely alone with any of them, because at night
they read or did their homework or listened to the
gramophone in their various 'dens'. Naturally she provided birthday parties, and as the years went on they
received Holy Communion and were confirmed, and
the sitting-room was full of framed, sometimes
coloured photographs of them to commemorate the
occasion. She would take turns as to who to have a set
on, one child or another, sometimes even her husband.

Then she would draw attention to what they were wearing and laugh at them and ask them to go and change or to please go and wash. Her word was law.

Her daughters did not resemble her, were not nearly so pretty. Her sons did have her colouring, so it was said. Not one of them was studious. Her daughters, especially her eldest daughter Maria, got moodier each year, and refused to eat anything except crisps and bananas. Tess said the child's father was to blame. Whenever they went to the city to shop they quarrelled because Maria chose dark, rather forlorn clothes and Tess would say it was no way for a young person to dress. Maria referred to her mother as The Duchess. It was a joke but not a welcome one.

It seemed no length at all till the eldest was due to go away to school, and Tess was studying prospectuses, buying uniforms, sewing on name-tapes and packing them off. If a child cried or snivelled, she would say 'Tis well for ye.' Equally when a tinker, or a horde of tinkers passed by the door she would say 'Sure they're happier than you or I', and close the shutters in the front room to discourage them from rapping on the window, a thing they did when the door-bell was not immediately answered. If they persisted, she sent the maid out with coppers, and to tell them to scoot. Meanwhile she would have her hands to her ears, saying the noise of the bell was driving her mad. Occasionally she suffered from sinus.

The first little lasting cloud to appear in Tess's life was when she turned forty and began to put on weight. She was soon having to have her dresses let out, and took to wearing smocks. Her husband said he had no objection. But had he? One night when he came home she got a distinct smell of cheap carnation scent, from his lapel. No, he had not been to the barber's, he had not been anywhere. He couldn't account for it and neither could she. Another occasion he couldn't exactly say what had detained him. She had rung the office, to be told by the new tactless secretary, that she was having a whale of a time, and that the boss had gone ages ago and was probably boozing. Yet an hour went by, and he had not appeared. His dinner had dried up and Tess had taken it in and out of the oven various times. He came in with a bit of grass between his teeth, chewing it. The pupils of his eyes were big and jet black.

The cat was out of the bag when, the following Sunday, one of the 'beauties' ran up to him in the church grounds, and offered him a peppermint sweet. They were two girls from another area who had come to open a boutique, and were 'man-mad'. They wore red a lot, were conspicuous miles off; and along with being identical in appearance, had the same ingratiating voices. One of them – and she could not tell which – had the gall to ring Tess up and invite her husband to the Mass, that they were having offered in their new premises. Tess wrote it down on the 'messages' pad and didn't refer to it when he came in. He attended the Mass the next evening, and as he admitted to her during their big reconciliation when he almost crushed her ribs, his heart was cut in two when he stood up for the gospel. He had never deceived her before and would never again. After the gospel he made a show of himself by leaving and came home with his head down and just sat in the front room smoking and staring at her, and now and then asking to be forgiven.

His next gift to her was the biggest gift of all – a mink

stole. She wore it to dress dances and used to say to the ladies that admired it, that it was much warmer than wool. Then she would hit it, or toss it into a chair, and imply that it meant nothing to her. But at home it was kept in a plastic bag on the top of the wardrobe, where no child could reach it, when playing charades or improvising fancy dress. When her husband began to follow the hunt, she would drive him to the meet, get out of the car, wrap the stole around her neck, and accept a sherry or a hot bouillon and chat with one of the new Lords or Ladies he was getting acquainted with. They lost friends and made friends. Even the girls from the boutique tried to worm their way into her life by asking her to play badminton, but Tess declined and gave them a small donation towards a cup. She would make joking references to them how their prices were diabolical, or that they would be left on the shelf, and find no husband. He made no comment as if they were complete strangers to him.

One September after another, a child went off to boarding school, and as time went on the house began to grow quiet, and there were no piles of dirty clothing in the big rush basket on the landing; her husband would take his time about coming home in the evenings, and she would read a book, or try to read a book, and register the clock striking each quarter, and wish that people would call to tell her that she was pretty, or to eat some of her legendary sandwiches, or to give her the little titbits of news. No such luck. People went to the houses of younger couples as they had once flocked to hers, and her husband though up to no monkey business was no longer quite the same, did not surprise her with little half-pound boxes of chocolates, did not whistle when she came down the stairs dressed to go out. He was busy with his various commitments, had meetings two or three evenings a week and on Sundays followed the hounds.

She had time on her hands, time to pluck her eyebrows, time to brood. The children wrote letters, mostly about the food, or the harsh conditions in their school, or some little surprise such as being given a toffee apple for a feast. She found her daughter's old diary and was a little shocked when she read 'Mammy is as usual smarmy, but Daddy does not see through her.' She could not say that it was then, no more than it was the moment when she smelt the cheap perfume on his lapel, nor the nausea when she read the disgusting magazine article about sex; it was not any of these events and yet they foreshadowed it.

One night her husband was sound asleep and for no reason she remembered one of her children, her favourite child, who had taken a fit, because he had seen a man, a horned devil, in black, inside the window pane. She herself had not seen it but she remembered her son's agitation and how she had not been able to quieten him. It was beyond her. Her husband was beside her, warm, his face almost babyish and she had no idea what he thought anymore, either sleeping or waking. Her children, her friends, her younger sister who had grown odd, and become attached to nature, all these people seemed to vibrate with more life, more urgency, even more desperation concerning the things they did. She felt odd, lonely, she felt afraid. Perhaps the manes of her dear dead aunt were at last coming to disquiet her. It was all in order – the same dinner each day of the week, the same night set aside for brief and unrenewing intercourse, the same grocery order on Saturday, the same humouring of the maid on Monday morning after the dance, the same the same the same It was as if she had just stepped onto ice.

'Oh Jesus,' she uttered aloud. 'Is this how it is when one begins to be unhappy.' She hadn't slept for four nights, not since the new plant had been installed in the chipboard factory. The noise and the incessancy of it followed her around the house all day and followed her to her bed at night. She cursed machinery. In her mind were the various outlandish solutions such as asking the foremen to stop it, such as stuffing her ears with little plugs of cotton wool, such as moving to a bungalow outside the town, such as. She closed her eyes tight so that all of her sensibilities were like two burning coals crammed into her little head, and she knew then that the smugness that had always been hers was something about to be taken away. She was shorn. For no reason she stole out of bed crept across the room and in the eerie chill, lifting the fawn curtain, she stared ahead at the blankness within the window pane.

Her husband found her laughing. She had just smashed a hand-mirror and was gloating over the seven years' bad luck in store. He did not know what to say. He had seen it come.

'What is it?' he said softly.

'What is it,' she said and her tone was like slivers, and she went on laughing at what she had just done.

The Creature

She was always referred to as The Creature by the townspeople, the dressmaker for whom she did buttonholing, the sacristan, who used to search for her in the pews on the dark winter evenings before locking up, and even the little girl Sally, for whom she wrote out the words of a famine song. Life had treated her rottenly, yet she never complained but always had a ready smile, so that her face with its round rosy cheeks, was more like something you could eat or lick; she reminded me of nothing so much as an apple fritter.

I used to encounter her on her way from devotions or from Mass, or having a stroll, and when we passed she smiled, but she never spoke, probably for fear of intruding. I was doing a temporary teaching job in a little town in the west of Ireland and soon came to know that she lived in a tiny house facing a garage that was also the town's undertaker. The first time I visited her, we sat in the parlour and looked out on the crooked lettering on the door. There seemed to be no one in attendance at the station. A man helped himself to petrol. Nor was there any little muslin curtain to obscure the world, because, as she kept repeating, she had washed it that very day and what a shame. She gave me a glass of rhubarb wine, and we shared the same chair, which was really a wooden seat with a latticed wooden back, that she had got from a rubbish heap and had varnished herself. After varnishing, she had dragged a nail over the wood to give a sort of mottled effect, and you could see where her hand had shaken, because the lines were wavery.

I had come from another part of the country; in fact, I had come to get over a love affair, and since I must have emanated some sort of sadness she was very much at home with me and called me 'dearest' when we met and when we were taking leave of one another. After correcting the exercises from school, filling in my diary, and going for a walk, I would knock on her door and then sit with her in the little room almost devoid of furniture – devoid even of a plant or a picture – and oftener than not I would be given a glass of rhubarb wine and sometimes a slice of porter cake. She lived alone and had done so for seventeen years. She was a widow and had two children. Her daughter was in Canada; the son lived about four miles away. She had not set eyes on him for the seventeen years – not since his wife had slung her out – and the children that she had seen as babies were big now, and, as she heard, marvellously handsome. She had a pension and once a year made a journey to the southern end of the country, where her relatives lived in a cottage looking out over the Atlantic.

Her husband had been killed two years after their marriage, shot in the back of a lorry, in an incident that was later described by the British Forces as regrettable. She had had to conceal the fact of his death and the manner of his death from her own mother, since her mother had lost a son about the same time, also in combat, and on the very day of her husband's funeral, when the chapel bells were ringing and re-ringing, she had to pretend it was for a travelling man, a tinker, who had died suddenly. She got to the funeral at the very last minute on the pretext that she was going to see the priest.

She and her husband had lived with her mother. She reared her children in the old farmhouse, eventually told her mother that she, too, was a widow, and as women together they worked and toiled and looked after the stock and milked and churned and kept a sow to whom she gave the name of Bessie. Each year the bonhams would become pets of hers, and follow her along the road to Mass or whenever and to them, too, she gave pretty names. A migrant workman helped in the summer months, and in the autumn he would kill the pig for their winter meat. The killing of the pig always made her sad, and she reckoned she could hear those roars – each successive roar – over the years, and she would dwell on that, and then tell how a particular naughty pig stole into the house one time and lapped up the bowls of cream and then lay down on the floor, snoring and belching like a drunken man. The workman slept downstairs on the settle bed, got drunk on Saturdays, and was the cause of an accident; when he was teaching her son to shoot at targets, the boy shot off three of his own fingers. Otherwise, her life had passed without incident.

When her children came home from school, she cleared half the table for them to do their exercises – she was an untidy woman – then every night she made blancmange for them, before sending them to bed. She used to colour it red or brown or green as the case may be, and she marvelled at these colouring essences almost as much as the children themselves did. She knitted two sweaters each year for them – two identical sweaters of bowneen wool – and she was indeed the proud mother when her son was allowed to serve at Mass.

Her finances suffered a dreadful setback when her entire stock contracted foot-and-mouth disease, and to add to her grief she had to see the animals that she so loved die and be buried around the farm, wherever they happened to stagger down. Her lands were disinfected and empty for over a year, and yet she scraped enough to send her son to boarding school and felt lucky in that she got a reduction of the fees because of her reduced circumstances. The parish priest had intervened on her behalf. He admired her and used to joke her on account of the novelettes she so cravenly read. Her children left, her mother died, and she went through a phase of not wanting to see anyone – not even a neighbour – and she reckoned that was her Garden of Gethsemane. She contracted shingles, and one night, dipping into the well for a bucket of water, she looked first at the stars then down at the water and thought how much simpler it would be if she were to drown. Then she remembered being put into the well for sport one time by her brother, and another time having a bucket of water douched over her by a jealous sister, and the memory of the shock of these two experiences and a plea to God made her draw back from the well and hurry up through the nettle garden to the kitchen, where the dog and the fire, at least, awaited her. She went down on her knees and prayed for the strength to press on.

Imagine her joy when, after years of wandering, her son returned from the city, announced that he would become a farmer, and that he was getting engaged to a local girl who worked in the city as a chiropodist. Her gift to them was a patchwork quilt and a special border of cornflowers she planted outside the window, because the bride-to-be was more than proud of her violet-blue eyes and referred to them in one way or another whenever she got the chance. The Creature thought how nice it would be to have a border of complementary flowers outside the window, and how fitting, even though *she* preferred wallflowers, both for their smell and their softness. When the young couple came home from the honeymoon, she was down on her knees weeding the bed of flowers, and, looking up at the young bride in her veiled hat, she thought, an oil painting was no lovelier or no more sumptuous. In secret, she hoped that her daughter-in-law might pare her corns after they had become intimate friends.

Soon, she took to going out to the cowshed to let the young couple be alone, because even by going upstairs she could overhear. It was a small house, and the bedrooms were directly above the kitchen. They quarrelled constantly. The first time she heard angry words she prayed that it be just a lovers' quarrel, but such spiteful things were said that she shuddered and remembered her own dead partner and how they had never exchanged a cross word between them. That night she dreamed she was looking for him, and though others knew of his whereabouts they would not guide her. It was not long before she realized that her daughter-in-law was cursed with a sour and grudging nature. A woman who automatically bickered over everything – the price of eggs, the best potato plants to put down, even the fields that should be pasture and those that should be reserved for tillage. The women got on well enough during the day, but rows were inevitable at night when the son came in and, as always, The Creature went out to the cowshed or down the road while things transpired. Up in her bedroom, she put little swabs of cotton wool in her ears to hide whatever sounds might be forthcoming. The birth of their first child did everything to exacerbate the young woman's nerves, and after three days the milk went dry in her breasts. The son called his mother out to the shed, lit a cigarette for himself, and told her that unless she signed the farm and the house over to him he would have no peace from his young barging wife.

This The Creature did soon after, and within three months she was packing her few belongings and walking away from the house where she had lived for fifty-eight of her sixty years. All she took was her clothing, her Aladdin lamp, and a tapestry denoting ships on a hemp-coloured sea. It was an heirloom. She found lodgings in the town and was the subject of much curiosity, then ridicule, because of having given her farm over to her son and daughter-in-law. Her son defected on the weekly payments he was supposed to make, but though she took the matter to her solicitor, on the appointed day she did not appear in court and as it happened spent the entire night in the chapel, hiding in the confessional.

Hearing the tale over the months, and how The Creature had settled down and made a soup most days, was saving for an electric blanket, and much preferred winter to summer, I decided to make the acquaintance of her son, unbeknownst to his wife. One evening I followed him to the field where he was driving a tractor. I found a sullen, middle-aged man, who did not condescend to look at me but proceeded to roll his own cigarette. I recognized him chiefly by the three missing fingers and wondered pointlessly what they had done with them on that dreadful day. He was in the long field where she used to go twice daily with buckets of separated milk, to feed the suckling calves. The house was to be seen behind some trees, and either because of secrecy or nervousness he got off the tractor, crossed over and stood beneath a tree, his back balanced against the knobbled trunk. It was a little hawthorn and, somewhat superstitious, I hesitated to stand under it. Its flowers gave a certain dreaminess to that otherwise forlorn place. There is something gruesome about ploughed earth, maybe because it suggests the grave.

He seemed to know me and he looked, I thought distastefully at my patent boots and my tweed cape. He said there was nothing he could do, that the past was the past, and that his mother had made her own life in the town. You would think she had prospered or remarried, his tone was so caustic when he spoke of 'her own life'. Perhaps he had relied on her to die. I said how dearly she still held him in her thoughts, and he said that she always had a soft heart and if there was one thing in life he hated it was the sodden handkerchief.

With much hedging, he agreed to visit her, and we arranged an afternoon at the end of that week. He called after me to keep it to myself, and I realized that he did not want his wife to know. All I knew about his wife was that she had grown withdrawn, that she had had improvements made on the place – larger windows and a bathroom installed – and that they were never seen together, not even on Christmas morning at chapel.

By the time I called on The Creature that eventful day, it was long after school, and, as usual, she had left the key in the front door for me. I found her dozing in the armchair, very near the stove, her book still in one hand and the fingers of the other hand fidgeting as if she were engaged in some work. Her beautiful embroidered shawl was in a heap on the floor, and the first thing she did when she wakened was to retrieve it and dust it down. I could see that she had come out in some sort of heat rash, and her face resembled nothing so much as a frog's, with her little raisin eyes submerged between pink swollen lids.

At first she was speechless; she just kept shaking her head. But eventually she said that life was a crucible, life was a crucible. I tried consoling her, not knowing what exactly I had to console her about. She pointed to the back door and said things were kiboshed from the very moment he stepped over that threshold. It seems he came up the back garden and found her putting the finishing touches to her hair. Taken by surprise, she reverted to her long-lost state of excitement and could say nothing that made sense. 'I thought it was a thief,' she said to me, still staring at the back door, with her cane hanging from a nail there.

When she realized who he was, without giving him time to catch breath, she plied both food and the drink on him, and I could see that he had eaten nothing, because the ox tongue in its mould of jelly was still on the table, untouched. A little whisky bottle lay on its side, empty. She told me how he'd aged and that when she put her hand up to his grey hairs he backed away from her as if she'd given him an electric shock. He who hated the soft heart and the sodden handkerchief must have hated that touch. She asked for photos of his family, but he had brought none. All he told her was that his daughter was learning to be a mannequin, and she put her foot in it further by saying there was no need to gild the lily. He had newspapers in the soles of his shoes to keep out the damp, and she took off those

lamp shoes and tried polishing them. I could see how
t all had been, with her jumping up and down trying
o please him but in fact just making him edgy. 'They
were drying on the range,' she said, 'when he picked
hem up and put them on.' He was gone before she
could put a shine on them, and the worst thing was that
ne had made no promise concerning the future. When
he asked 'Will I see you?' he had said 'Perhaps,' and
he told me that if there was one word in the English
vocabulary that scalded her, it was the word 'perhaps'.
'I did the wrong thing,' I said, and, though she didn't
nod, I knew that she also was thinking it – that secretly
he would consider me from then on a meddler. All at
once I remembered the little hawthorn tree, the bare
ploughed field, his heart as black and unawakened as
he man I had come away to forget, and there was re-
eased in me, too, a gigantic and useless sorrow. Where-
us for twenty years she had lived on that last high
ightrope of hope, it had been taken away from her,
eaving her without anyone, without anything, and I
wished that I had never punished myself by applying to
be a sub in that stagnant, godforsaken little place.

Honeymoon

Elizabeth knew that honeymoons were likely to be fraught, and were not the pleasant occasions that the send-off of rice, or confetti suggested. She remembered a cousin who had to be taken to hospital for an operation for haemorrhoids after hers, and another girl whose husband had conked her with a beach ball, whereby she had to have six stitches, and still another man – middle aged – who ordered plates and plates of oysters the better to consummate his marriage and at the end of two weeks declared he was still a bachelor.

Her honeymoon was different in that she had lived with the man in question for six months before actually becoming married to him. The reason was that he had difficulties in securing his divorce. Then, when it did take place, the marriage itself was so like none other, since it passed without a Mass or relatives or a wedding breakfast, or anything that could be called celebration. It was in the sacristy of a chapel on a weekday with two strangers – builders – as witnesses, and the ceremony presided over by an elderly and somewhat disgruntled priest. Theirs was a mixed marriage, which was why it took place in a sacristy and the parish priest as much as told her that it would not last.

The honeymoon came months later, after he had

fixed up the old sports car and secured a workman to keep an eye to the sheep scattered over the mountainy farm. The little sports car was in perfect working order and they set off with the hood down. Soon they passed the poor hungry fields and descended the narrow rough road towards the valley, towards houses and pasture land and green hedges saying good-bye for a while to their own single-storied white-cemmed lodge, to the grim mountain and to the lake where he had set a trap to catch pike. Down in the valley it was warm and sunny, and she remembered her own home and her own childhood as she saw the clothes on the line, and the women painting piers, and the little children waving endlessly at whatever passed. Although it was only six months since she had eloped with him, that part of her life seemed far away, and almost forbidden to her, to recall. And still it resided in her, somewhere, her parents' cut-stone house, the big empty rooms with the blond blinds drawn through the summer days, the hosts of daffodils, and the one narcissus in a dead child's hand, and once the soft tar on the road ruining a pair of white canvas shoes that had been given her.

From time to time he would ask her to look at the map, or pronounce the name of a town they were about to approach; and when they had driven for about three hours he decided that they should stop for tea. They stopped in a town where there had once been a dreadful battle and she told him what she remembered of it, from her schooldays. He was not a native and sometimes she got the feeling that he had no pity for those people, her people, who had for so long lived in subjugation and who like her were ashamed to confront themselves. He was twice her age, and she obeyed him in everything, even in the type of shoes she was to wear

– completely flat shoes which as it happened gave her a
pain in her instep.

The tea turned out to be delicious, what with home
made bread, tart, barely-ripened tomatoes, and salmon
that had been cooked in muslin. Setting out again they
were almost gay, as if no great divide of age or tem
perament lay between them. He had had two other
wives of different nationalities and she often wondered
if they were as biddable and obedient as herself. In
this she despised herself because at heart she was quite
wilful and rebellious and her earliest memory was of
herself refusing to remember the names of grown-up
people whom she resented. She had developed these
traits of niceness and agreeableness simply to get away
from people – to keep them from pestering her.

The first night they slept in the car, in a hay field,
alongside a river. The smell of newly-mown hay possessed the air, and what with that, and the gurgle of the
river, and the birds roosting in the trees, and now and
then a car or a lorry on the main road, they found it
hard to get a wink of sleep at all. They were wakened
by crows in the very early morning, and were up and
on their way to secure a can of milk long before the
farm woman had rounded up her two cows.

They set out soon after breakfast and passed a little
town where he bought fishing flies and a pound of eating apples. Before long they entered that part of the
country where there were hedges of fuchsia, and consequently they were greeted by the dangling earrings
of vivid red no matter where they looked. She felt like
adorning herself with them. They parked the car and
crossed some fields down to an ancient fort, where they
encountered an old woman, a caretaker, from whom
they had to get the big key.

On the spur of the moment, and for no reason, this woman asked them if they would like to rent a cottage, and just as rashly he agreed. The cottage belonged to her daughter and she gave them exact instructions where to find it. To enter the fort they had to stoop and once inside it was damp and grimy, with grey powdery stone peeling out of the walls, and a strange intimation of some other life, a relentless life that had gone on here.

The woman watched them, wrapt in curiosity, as if something weird might happen, or as if once, some other visitor had been compelled to do something untoward there. Obviously she hated her job and was doing it only out of necessity. She had no historical information whatsoever and said the place couldn't be worse for her sciatica.

When they arrived at the daughter's cottage they were delighted that it overlooked the sea and that there were great sweeps of sand, fine black sand; an uncanny smooth black vista like none that she had ever seen. The loose grains crept along the surface of it, playing an endless game. As they knocked on the open door, the shy daughter crawled out from under a table, a hunchbacked figure, in silver shoes, wearing a richly embroidered shawl. Her delight in seeing them was matched only by her agitation and she kept saying 'yes sir' before being asked anything at all. They crossed a little kitchen garden disturbing a hen who was on the point of laying, entered a little paddock where a goat was tethered, to reach the cottage that was smothered in roses and shrubs. All the time Rose clapped her hands and kept saying 'ha-ha'. The cottage comprised two rooms, a huge bare swept hearth, a low bamboo

97

table and a churn resting on its side, which was as she
said an antique. There was a single iron bed and the
floor exhaled steam and damp. The hunchback saw
them look at each other, shake their heads and as they
declined she threw some evil word at them. Her vexa-
tion was as vivid as moments before her excitement had
been. Then she pelted stones after them, and told
them to get out of her sight.

That night, their sleep was less restless because of
becoming more accustomed to the outdoors, the
sounds, the smells, and the cramped environment of
the car, with its little sponge mattress. In the morning
he decided to do some fishing and they were able to
follow the source of the river from the very spot where
they were parked. Though sad at being left alone Elizabeth was pleased to see him set off, in his thigh-high
wellington boots, with his new rod, and his lid of
newly-dug wriggling worms. She folded the mattress,
washed the breakfast things, ate some chocolate, and
then sat down with the intention of talking to herself,
and telling herself little stories to pass the time. She
could hear the river, and tried to make out what sort
of words it was saying to itself, and once she ran across
to take a look at the brown water and the stones that
were richly covered in a green luxurious moss. The
time just crawled by, and she thought of snails and
wished that she were one, and wondered about the
little child she felt certain was in her; and what its sex
was likely to be. She plaited her hair, then sat facing
the sun, staring directly ahead at the two houses, the
only two, about a mile distant, on a hill. They were
identical houses of grey stone, with very blue slates, and
red hall doors. She took to thinking of the occupants
and wondered if they were friends, and if they had

children, and if so, how they got to and from school.
Just then a man appeared from the road-side with a
sack of flour on his back, and she said hello almost at
the exact same moment as he did. He commented on
the fine weather and seeing that she smiled, he put
down the sack and started to look at the little car and
to touch the headlights. Then he stooped down and
looked inside it. He was intrigued by it. She leant in
and turned on the wireless and within seconds he was
clapping his hands to the music, and letting out a yodel
as if he were a guest at a house dance. She conveyed him
across the field, and he told her how he lived with his
wife Nora and how she pined for company, and how
the previous summer hikers had called on them and
taken tea with them. She was on the point of turning
back when he asked if she would like to come up and
meet Nora. He badly wanted her to go, so she went
both to please him and to inspect one of the two houses
that a short while before had been like a house in a
mystery story, never to be entered.

She had to take off her shoes, as they crossed the
various little brooks. Some stones carried the timeworn
footprints of people and animals. One stone had the
shape of a heel in it and he told her it was there since
he was a small child. As they approached the house he
called Nora, in a high excited voice, and a youngish
woman came running down the steps, wiping her
hands on her apron. The moment she saw he was not
alone, she quit smiling, and began to pant, and drew
her long tongue out and raised it to the tip of her nose,
touching her nose over and over again, making some
important signal with it, and demanding of him to do
the exact same thing. They looked identical, like

brother and sister, having the same lugubrious features, the same gravel eyes, and these elongated tongues, with which they could touch the tips of their noses. Once inside the house Nora began to jump up and down, throw cutlery, splash water, and whimper so that the man was obliged to take her to the next room where they spent several minutes.

When they emerged the woman was calm, but reserved, shook hands with her guest, put a newspaper on the chair, made tea in a china pot, and left it to draw in the middle of the kitchen floor, well away from coals or sparks from the fire. She gabbled on about what a nice day it was, and how it was Tuesday, St Anthony's day, and how hikers had called the summer before and would call again. He told her about the little blonde sports car, the mudguard, the headlights, and the dashboard with the various knobs of light; and then he told her about the radio and the tunes that came pouring out of it, like milk out of the separator, he said. She jumped up and down, took off her skull cap, threw it in the air and started to dance with joy. They proposed that after milking time, they would come down and visit the little car, and listen to the wireless. They shook both her hands when she left, repeated the arrangements, and said they would bring a bottle of milk and a jug of cream.

Elizabeth headed down the lane, over the field, across the various brooks, and down the last soggy field to where she knew her husband would be waiting. As she approached she saw a herd of cattle centred round the car, some lowing, some making louder, more ominous noises and she picked up a few rocks in case she be accosted.

Her husband called to her, to please hurry and asked where on earth she had got herself to. A small black bull was butting its way through the radiator, while some other members of the herd were sampling the canvas hood, licking it with their thick, pink tongues. She shouted out to her husband that she was afraid. He repeated that she had better hurry, since the car was in danger of being slashed and gored, and throwing two rocks somewhat rashly and randomly she managed to make three of the animals rear up towards the mudguard, and make her passage to the door all the more treacherous. Just then he began to blow the hooter, mercilessly; and shocked by the implosion and obviously unaccustomed to it, the cattle shied away, and scattered in all directions, enabling her to get in.

He asked what she meant, disappearing like that, with some strange yokel. The bull was still adhering to the radiator, and starting up the car he had to battle his way, forcing the animal back on its hind legs, and finally capsizing it altogether. The last she saw were the animals, like a raging swarm, threatening to chase them as they drove out of the field, and then she remembered how they could not leave because of the promise she had made. She told him about the visitors, and their identical faces, and he said how very interesting as he drove on. She thought of sundown, and their excitement, she even pictured them coming hand in hand, down the lane and across the stepping stones, probably dressed up, and she imagined their disappointment and then she thought how she had thought that her own husband was a man she had loved, but that she had been mistaken, and she remembered the phrase 'marry in haste, repent at leisure' and

she began to cry quietly and unobtrusively, and yet she
cried from the very depth of her young, and about to
be chastised, being.

A Journey

February the twenty-second. Not far away was the honking of water fowl in the pond at Battersea Park. The wrong side of London some said, but she liked it and the pale green power station was her landmark, as once upon a time a straggle of blue hills had been. The morning was cold, the ice had clawed at the window and left its tell-tale marks – lines – long jagged lines, criss-cross scrawls, lines at war with one another, lines bent on torment. It was still like twilight in the bedroom and yet she wakened with alertness, and her heart was as warm as a little ball of knitting wool. He was deep in a trough of sleep, impervious to nudging, to hitting, to pounding. He was beautiful. His hair, like a halo, was arced around his head – beautiful hair, not quite brown, not quite red, not quite gold, of the same darkness as gunmetal but with strands of brightness. Oh Christ he'll think he's in his own house with his own woman she thought as his eyelids flickered and he peered through. But he didn't. He knew where he was and said how glad he was to be there, and drawing her towards him he held her and squeezed her out like a bit of old washing. They were off to Scotland, he to deliver a lecture to some students and later to men, fellow unionists who worked on the shipyards.

'We're going a-travelling,' she said almost doubtfully.

'Yes pet.'

At any rate he hadn't changed his mind yet. He was a great vacillator.

She made the coffee while he contemplated getting up, and from the kitchen she kept urging him, saying how they would be late, how he must please bestir himself. For some reason she was reminded of her wedding morning, both mornings had a feeling of unreality, the same uncertainty plus her anxiety about being late. But that was a long time ago. That was over, and dry in the mouth like a pod or a desiccated cud. This was this. This man upstairs, why do I love him she thought. A working man, shy and moody and inarticulate, a man unaccustomed to a woman like her. They hardly talked. Not that speech was what mattered between people. She learnt that the very day she had accosted him in a train a few weeks before. She saw him and simply had to communicate with him, touched the newspaper he was scanning, flicked it ever so lightly with her finger, and he stared across at her and very quietly admitted her into his presence, but without a word without even a face-saving hello.

'I can't say things,' he had said and then breathed out quickly and nervously as if it had cost him a lot to admit. He was like a hound, a little whippet. It was like crossing the Rubicon. Also daft. Also dicey. A journey of pain. She had no idea then how extensive that journey would be. A good man? Maybe. Maybe not. She was looking for reasons to unlove him. When he came down he almost, but didn't smile. There was such a tentativeness to him. Is it always going to be like this she thought, spilling the coffee, slopping it in the saucer and then nervously dumping the brown granular mass from a strainer onto an ashtray.

'I have no composure,' she said. From him another wan smile. Would her buying the tickets be all right, would he look away while she paid, would it be an auspicious trip? She took his hand, and warmed it and said she never wanted to do aught else, and he said not to say such things, not to say them, but in fact they were only a skimming of the real things she was longing to say. Years divided them, class divided them, position divided them. He wanted to give her a present and couldn't in case it wasn't swish enough. He bought perfume off a hawker in Oxford Circus, offered it to her and then took it back. Probably gave it to his woman, put it down on the table along with his pay packet. Or maybe left it on a dressing table, if they had one. A tender moment? All these unknowns divided them. The morning that she was getting married, he was pruning trees in an English park, earning a smallish sum and living with a woman who had four children. He had always lived with some woman or another, but insisted that he wasn't a philanderer, wasn't. He lived with Madge, now, drank two pints of beer every evening, cuddled his baby and smoked forty cigarettes a day.

In the taxi he whispered to her, to please not look at him like that, and at the airport he spent the bulk of the waiting time in the gents. She wondered if there wasn't a barbers in there, or if perhaps, he hadn't done a disappearing act, like people on their wedding day who do not show up at the altar rails. In fact he had bought a plastic hairbrush to straighten his hair for the journey because it had got tangled in the night. Afterwards he put it in her travel bag. Did she need a travel bag? How long were they to stay? No knowing. They were terribly near and they were not near. No outsider could guess the relationship. In the plane, the hostess tried hard to flirt with him, said she'd seen him on television but he was shy and skirted the subject by asking for a light. He was very active with his union and often appeared on television debates; at private meetings he exhorted the members to rope in new ones. He had made quite a reputation for himself by reading them cases from history and clippings from old newspapers, making them realize how they had been treated for hundreds of years. He was a scaffolder like his father before him, but he left Belfast soon after his parents died. His brothers and sisters were scattered.

When they got to their destination he suddenly suggested that she dump the bag in a safety locker, and she knew then that she shouldn't have brought it, and that possibly they would not be staying overnight. Walking up the street of Edinburgh with a bitter breeze in their faces she pointed to a castle that looked like a dungeon and asked him what he thought of it. Not much. He didn't think much – that was his answer. What did he do – dream, daydream, imagine, forget. The leaves in the municipal flower-bed were blowing and shivering, mere tatters, but the soil was a beautiful flaky black. They happened to be passing a funeral parlour and she asked if he preferred burial or cremation but about that too he was tepid and indifferent. It made no matter. They should still be in bed, under covers, cogitating. She linked him and he jerked his arm saying those who knew him, knew the woman he lived with, and he would not like it to appear otherwise. They were halfway up the hill, and there was between them now, one of those little swords of silence that is always slicing love, or that kind of love.

'If Madge knew about this, she'd be immeasurably hurt,' he said.

'But Madge will know,' she thought, but did not say. She said instead that it was colder up North, that they were not far from the sea, and didn't he detect bits of hail in the wind. He saw the sadness, traced it lightly with his finger, traced the near tears and the little pouch under the lids. He said 'You're a terrible woman altogether,' to which she replied 'You're not a bad bloke,' and they laughed. He was supposed to have travelled by train the night before, the very night when he slept with her and had his hair pulled from the roots. How good a liar was he and how strong a man? He had crossed the street ahead of her and to make amends he waited for her across the road, waited by the lights, and watched her, admiring, as she came across, watched her walk, her lovely legs, her long incongruous skirt and watched the effect she had on others, one of shock as if she was undressed or carrying some sort of invisible torch. He referred to an ancient queen and her carriage.

'It's not that it's not pleasant holding your arm,' he said, and took her elbow feeling the wobble of the funny bone. Then he had to make a phone call, and soon they were going somewhere, in a taxi, and the back streets of Edinburgh were not unlike the back streets of any other town, a bit black, a bit drowsy and pub fronts being washed down.

'He's afraid of me,' she thought. 'And I'm afraid of him,' and fear is corrosive, and she felt certain that the woman he lived with was probably much more adept at living and arguing, would make him bring in the coal, or clean out the ashes or share his last cigarette, would put her cards on the table. For a moment she was seized with longing to see them together, and had a terrible idea that she would call as a travelling saleswoman with a little attaché case, full of cleaning stuffs so as she would have to go in and show her wares. She would see their kitchen and their pram and the baby in it, she would see how tuned they were to one another. But that was not necessary, because he was leaving because it had all gone dry and flaccid, between him and the woman it was all over. When he looked at her then it was a true felt look, and it was laden with sweetness, white, mesmerizing like the blossom that hangs from the cherry trees.

Before addressing the first batch of students he called on some friends. Even that was furtive, he didn't knock, but whistled some sort of code through the letter box. In the big, sparsely furnished room there was a pregnant cat, marmalade, and the leftovers of a breakfast, and a man and a woman who had obviously just tumbled out of their bed. She thought this is how it should be. When, through a crack in the kitchen door, catching a glimpse of their big tossed bed and the dented pillows without pillow-slips, she ached to go in and lie there, and she knew that the sight of it had permeated her consciousness and that it was a longing she would always feel. That longing was replaced by a stitch in the chest, then a lot of stitches, and then something like a lump in the back of the mouth, something that would not dissolve. Would he live with her like he said. Would he do it. Would he forsake everything, fear, respectability, safeness, the woman, the child? The questions were like pendulums swinging this way and that. The answers would swing too.

The woman she had just met was called Ita and the

man was called Jim the Limb. He had some defect in his right arm. They were plump and radiant, what with their night, and their big breakfast and now a fresh pot of tea. They were chain smokers. Ita said her fur coat and the marmalade cat were alike, and he, her lover, said that probably that was a wrong thing to say. But there was no wrong thing as far as she was concerned. She just wanted them to welcome her in, to accept her. When they talked about the union, and the various men, and the weekly meetings, when they discussed a rally that was to take place later in London she thought, 'Let me be one of you, let me put aside my old stupid flitting life, let me take part, let me in.' Her life was not exactly soigné and she too had lived in small rooms and ridden a ridiculous bicycle, and swapped old shoes for other old shoes, but she seemed not to belong, because she had bettered herself, had done it on her own, and now that she was a graphic designer, she designed alone. Also these were townspeople, they all had lived in small steep houses, slept two or three or four to a bed, sparred, lived in and out of one another's pockets, knew familiarity well enough to know that it was the only hope. Ita announced that she was not going to the factory that morning, said dammit, the bloody sweatshop, and told him of two women who were fired because they had gone deaf from the machines and weren't able to hear proper. He said they must fight it. They were a clan. Yet, when he winked at her he seemed to be saying something else, something ambiguous, and saying 'I see you there, I am not forsaking you,' or was he saying, 'Look how influential I am, look at me.' A word he often used was big-shot. Maybe he had dreams of being a big-shot?

Just before the four of them left the house for the

college he went for the third time to the lavatory and she believed he had gone to be sick. Yet when he stood on the small ladder platform, holding up a faulty loud-speaker, brandishing it, making jokes about it – calling it Big Brother he seemed to be utterly in his element. He spoke without notes, he spoke freely, telling the crowd of his background in Belfast, his father's work on the shipyards, his having to emigrate, his job in London, the lads, the way this fellow or that fellow had got nabbed, and though what he had to say was about victimization he made it all funny. When questions were put it was clear that he had cajoled them all, except for one dissenter, an aristocratic-looking boy in a dress suit, a boy who seemed to be on the brink of a nervous breakdown. Even with that, he dealt deftly. He replied without any venom and when the dissenter was booed and told to belt up he said 'Aach' to his friends who were heckling. The hat was passed around, a navy college cap into which coins were tossed from all corners of the room. She hesitated; not knowing whether to give a lot, or a little, and wanting only to do the right thing. She gave a pound note, and afterwards in the refectory to where they had all repaired, she saw a girl hand him ten pounds and thought how the collection must have been to foot his expenses.

Ita and Jim decided to accompany them to the next city, where he was conducting the same sort of meeting, in the evening, in a public hall. Getting on the station late as they did, he said 'Let's jump in here,' and ushered them into a first-class carriage. When the ticket collector came, she paid the difference, knowing that he had chosen to go in there because he felt it was where she belonged. At first they couldn't hear one another for the rattle of the train, the shunting of other carriages, and a whipping wind that lashed through a broken window. He dozed, and sometimes coming awake he nudged her with his shoe. The ladies sat on one side, the men opposite, and Ita was whispering to her, in her ear, saying when she met Jim how they went to bed for a week and how she was so sore, and finally had to have stitches. He looked at the women whispering and tittering and he seemed to like that, and there was a satisfaction in the way he rocked and dozed.

They were all hungry.

'Starving you I am,' he said to her as he asked a porter for the name of a restaurant.

'A French joint,' he decided. As they settled themselves in the drab and garish room, Ita tripped over the flex of the table lamp. Jim glowered with embarrassment, said this wasn't home, and to behave herself. They dived into the basket of bread, calling for butter, butter. He made jokes about the wine, sniffed it and asked if for sure it was the best vintage, and knowing that he was shy and awkward with his fingers she fed him her little potato sticks from her plate. He accepted them like they were matches, and then gobbled them down, and the others knew what they had suspected, that this pair were lovers, and Jim said they looked like two people in a picture and they smiled as if they were in a picture and their faces scanned one another as if in a beautiful daze. At the meeting he gave the same speech, except that it had to be shortened, and this he did by omitting one anecdote about a man who was sent to jail for speaking Gaelic in the northern province of his own country. There was a second collection and the amounts subscribed were much higher, because the bulk of the audience were working men, and proud to contribute.

Afterwards they repaired to a big ramshackle room, at the top of a big house in the north side of the city. In the hall there were hundreds of milk bottles, and in the back hall two or three bicycles jumbled together. He had bought a bottle of whiskey, and in the kitchen she heated a kettle to make a hot punch for him because his throat was sore. He came in and told her what a grand person she was, and he kissed her stealthily. The kitchen was a shambles and although at first intending to tidy it a bit, all she did was scald two cups and a tumbler for his punch. Some had hot whiskey, some had cold, whereas she had hers laced in a cup of tea.

In the ramshackle room they all talked, interrupting one another, joking, having inside conversation about meetings they'd been to, and other meetings to which they'd sent hecklers, and demonstrations that they were planning to have and all their supporters in France, Italy and throughout. She looked up at the light shade, crinkled plastic, as big as a beach ball, and with a lot of dots. She felt useless. The designs she made were simple and geometric and somewhat stark, but at that moment they seemed irrelevant. They had no relation to these people, to their conversation, to their curious kind of bantering anger. She remembered nights on end when she had striven to make a shape or a design that would go straight to the quick of someone's being, she had done it alone, and she had gruelled over it but these people would think it a bit of a joke.

The place was slovenly but still it was a place. Several brass rings had come off their hooks and the heavy velvet curtain gaped. He was being witty. Some-one had said that there were more ways than one of killing a cat but he had intervened to say that it was 'skinning' a cat. That was the first flicker of cruelty that she saw in him. She was sitting next to him on the divan bed, she leaning back against the wall, slightly out of things, he pressing forward, positing the odd joke. He said that at forty he might find his true voca-tion in life, which was to be a whizz-kid. There was a rocking chair in which one of the men sat, and several easy chairs with stained and torn upholstery, their springs dipping down, to a variable degree depending on the weight and the colossal pranks of the sitters. Sometimes a girl with plaits would rush over and sit on her man's knee and pull his beard and then the springs dropped down like the inside of a broken melodion. If only he and she could be that unreserved.

Then he was missing, out on the landing using the phone. She knew they had missed the last plane, and long ago had missed the last train and that they would have to kip down somewhere, and she thought how awful if it had to be on a bench at a station or at a depot. Ita asked her if they were perhaps going to make a touring holiday, and she said no but couldn't add to that, couldn't gloss the reply with some extra little piece of information. When he came in he told her that a taxi was on its way.

'I don't know where we're heading for, Wonder-land,' he said, shaking hands with Ita and then he said cheers to the room at large.

The hotel was close to the airport, a modern build-ing made of concrete cubes, like something built by a child, and with vertical slits for windows. They might be turned away. He went in whistling. She waited, one foot on the step of the taxi and one on the footpath and said an involuntary prayer. She saw him handing over money, then beckoning for her to come in. He had signed the register and in the lift, as he fondled her, he told her the false name that he had used. It was a nice name, Egan. In the bedroom they thought of whiskey, and then of milk and then of milk and whiskey, but they were too tired, and shy all over again, and neither of them was impervious enough to give an order, while the other was listening.

'I know you better now,' he said. She wondered at what precise moment in the day had he come to know her better, had he crept in on her like a little invisible camera, and knew that he knew her, and would know her for all time. Maybe some non-moment, when she walked gauchely towards the ladies' room, or when asked her second name she hesitated, in case by giving a name she should compromise him.

She apologized for not talking more, and he said that was what was lovely about her, and he apologized for giving the same lecture twice, and for all the stupid things that got said. Then he trotted around naked, getting his tiny little transistor from his overcoat pocket, studying the hotel clock – a square face laid into the bedside table – trying the various lights. He had never stayed in a hotel before, and it was then he told her that there would be a refund if in the morning they didn't eat breakfast. He had paid. His earnings for the day had been swallowed up by it.

'I'll refund you,' she said, and he said what rot, and in the dark they were together again, together like spare limbs, like rag dolls, or bits of motor car tyre, bits of themselves, together, so effortless, and so fond, and with such harmony, as if they had grown up that way, always were and always would be. But she couldn't ask. It had to come from him. He was thinking of going back home, leaving London, changing jobs. Well, wherever he went, she was going too. He had brought everything to a head, everything she had wanted to feel, love and pity and softness and passion and patience and insatiable jealousy. They went to sleep talking, then half talking, voices trailing away like tendrils, sleepy voices, sleepy brains, sleepy bodies, talking, not talking, dumb.

'I love you, I love you,' he said it the very moment that the hotel clock triggered off, and all the doubts of the previous day and the endless cups of coffee, and the bulging ashtrays were all sweet reminders of a day in which the fates changed. He said he dearly wished that they could lie there for hours on end and have coffee and papers sent up and lie there and let the bloody aeroplanes and the bloody world go by. But why were they hurrying? It was a Saturday and he had no work.

'I'll say good-bye here,' he said, and he kissed her and pulled the lapel of her fur coat up around her neck so that she wouldn't feel the cold.

'But we're going together,' she said. He said yes but they would be in a public place and they would not be able to say good-bye, not intimately. He kissed her.

'We will be together?' she said.

'It will take time,' he said.

'How long?' she asked.

'Months, years . . .' They were ready to go.

In the plane they talked first about mushrooms and

she said how mushrooms were reputed to be magic, and then she asked him if he had wanted a son rather than a daughter, and he said no, a daughter, and smiled at the thought of his little one. He read four of the morning papers, read them, re-read them, combed the small news items that were put in at the last minute, and got printing ink all over his hands. The edges of the paper sometimes jutted against her nose, or her eye or her forehead and without turning he would say 'Sorry love'. To live with, he would be all right, silent at times, undemonstrative, then all of a sudden as touching as an infant. Every slight gesture of his, every 'Sorry love' tore at some place in her gut.

A bus was waiting on the tarmac, right next to the landed plane. He said they needn't bother rushing, and as a result they were very nearly not taken at all. In fact the steward looked down the aisle of the bus, put up a finger to say that there was room for one, and then in the end grumpily let them both enter. They had to sit separately, with an aisle between them and she began to revert to her cursed superstitions such as if they passed a white gate all would be fortunate between them.

At the terminus he had to make a phone call, and she could see him, although she had meant not to look, gesticulating fiercely in the glass booth. When he came out he was biting his thumb. After a while, he said he was late, that the woman had to stay home from work, that he was in the wrong again. She saw it very clearly, very cruelly, as clear and as cruel as the lines of ice that had claimed the window pane. Claims. Responsibility. Slogans. 'Be here be here.'

They walked up the road towards the underground

tation. No matter how she carried it the travel bag bumped against her, or when she changed hands, against him. He said she was never to tell anyone. She said she wasn't likely to go spouting it, and he said why the frown, why spoil everything with a frown like that. It went out like a shooting star, the sense of peace, the suffusion, the near-happiness. He asked her to hang on, while he got cigarettes, and then plunging into the dark passage that led to the underground, he saw her hesitate, and said did she always take taxis. They kissed. It was a dark unpropitious passage but a real kiss. Their mouths clung, the skins of their lips would not be parted, she felt that they might fall into a trance in order not to terminate it. He was as helpless then as a schoolboy, and his eyes as pathetic as watered ink. In some indefinable way, and whatever happened, he would be part of her for all time, an essence.

'If I must, if I must talk to you may I,' she said. He looked at her bitterly. He was like a chisel. 'I can't promise anything,' he said, and repeated it. Then he was gone, doing a little hop through the turnstile, and omitting to get a ticket. She walked on, the bag kept bumping off the calf of her leg; soon when she had enough poise she would hail a taxi. Would he go? Would he come back? What would he do? It was like a door that had just come ajar, and anything could happen to it, it could shut tight or open a fraction or fly open in a burst. She thought of the bigness and wonder of destiny, meeting him in a packed train had been a fluke, and this now was a fluke, and things would either convene to shut that door, or open it a little, or open and close it alternately, and they would be together, or not be together as life the gaffer thought fit.

Sisters

Every year their parents went to the horse show, and every year their father went on the batter, so that the visit had to be cut short and the distraught couple travelled home by train. Invariably he disgraced himself in the train, spent the three hours in the bar, and picked quarrels with people whom he had previously been buying drinks for. Every year he promised his wife that he would not break his pledge and she in turn promised her children that she would bring them back a present each. When they were younger the children used to be sent to an aunt or relatives, but as time went on they were allowed to stay at home, and Helen, the middle daughter was put in charge of the funds. There was a perpetual scarcity of money and even the tariff for the trip itself had to be borrowed until the harvest.

On the first day Helen gave a kind of party for their friends the Vaughans. Pançakes and cider were served out on the lawn. The lawn itself was pretty dishevelled, with high grass turning to hay, very sturdy devils pokers and some rose bushes that were long since submerged. Helen presided while her brother Teddy who was in love with Georgina – the oldest and most beautiful of the Vaughan girls – told little anecdotes and called people simply by their initial.

The pancakes tended to be burnt on the one side and as if to compensate for that were a raw eggy colour on the other. They were filled with jam and folded only once. Apart from fiddling at Georgina's lisle stocking Teddy kept pointing to a tall chestnut tree and saying that if only it could talk dire secrets could be revealed. He seemed to be implying that he had done dreadful things there, and his youngest sister Creena took to running off every other minute to say a prayer for purity. Eventually he told her to sit still and stop being so fidgety. Her older sister Peg took her part and said 'the little dote'. Peg and Creena were friends and allies, at loggerheads with Helen and Teddy, who were as it happened the glamorous, the important, the most favoured ones.

Throughout the party the Vaughan girls lay on the warm grass, folded their cardigans to serve as cushions and after being still for some time, the 'Beauty' got up and perched on her bicycle, so that her long legs were dangling down and her toeless sandals submerged in the grass. Teddy fed her a sandwich comprised of two chocolate biscuits. He said that in the morning he would fetch her mushrooms. It was a prodigal year for mushrooms and each morning the group set out, to the various fields, certain that their cans and their baskets would be full. Usually they went in pairs, Teddy with the Beauty, Helen with the Beauty's sister Bunny, Creena and Peg, and the two younger Vaughan children who ate grass as an example of how daring they were. Only that very morning Bunny did the splits out on a hill, and parted her legs so wide that there was conjecture that she might never be able to put them together again. Some scolded, some laughed, but Creena who was so frightened of the situation, took it to be a defiance of the laws of chastity and prayed to the Virgin to bring the girl's legs together again. Creena was always slow at sighting the mushrooms and was a complete laughing stock because that day, though standing next to a huge crop of them she had not seen them but had been concentrating instead on a weasel as it hissed from a burrow in the base of a tree. They nicknamed her Dopey for that. It was an amazement even to herself that she had not trod on this beautiful dome of them and when they were being divided up by Helen she was given only two and slightly blemished ones.

During the party Creena or Peg were often dispatched to the house to get another glass, or a cup, or simply to make themselves scarce while another secret was being unfolded between the ringleaders. It was decided that there would be a party three afternoons a week and a fancy-dress on the Sunday. They speculated about costumes, and Teddy bragged about sending to a theatrical hiring agency for a jockey's outfit, of saffron and brown. The Beauty decided that she would go as 'The Colleen Bawn' a drowned creature, whose body was washed up, and about whom rhyme and verses had been written. The party was brought to an abrupt end, because Hickey, the workman, came in from the fields, ravenous, and seeing them all lounging about the place, and seeing the state of the kitchen with burning frying pan, and spilt batter, he set about ejecting the Vaughans, telling them what snotty noses they were. Teddy intervened, reminded him that he was only a workman, whereupon Hickey picked him up, threw him over a paling, and told the world at large that such a twit had for a backside two eggs tied up in a handkerchief. In secret Creena laughed, because in his white flannels Teddy did look a trifle comic, and a trifle citified, compared with the other man in his big dark ganzy and his baggy trousers of dark serge.

That night no supper was served and in the morning Helen sent Creena and Peg to search for mushrooms while she stayed at home to wash her hair and give it a camomile rinse. They got half a can, which was less than their average, boiled them with milk, adding lots of salt and pepper to make a kind of broth. That constituted their lunch. There was no tea and no supper, because Helen who was in charge of the funds was saving to buy a watch. Teddy put on his blazer and announced that he had a standing invitation to the Vaughans, where no doubt he would be served mixed grill and whiskey. Helen was making her evening visit to the hospital, to visit Miss Bugler, a beautiful young woman who was being eaten away with a fatal disease. Helen went each evening taking flowers and provisions from Miss Bugler's elderly parents. They themselves went only on a Sunday because the visits were so distressing to them. During the week they pottered in their garden, or sat on the veranda and just before six old Mrs Bugler would sit down and write a verse to her daughter and pin it to the flowers. Their hollyhocks were renowned.

No sooner had she gone than Peg got into a flying temper and plotted with Creena the numerous methods by which they could and would kill Helen. Helen had got the job of going to the hospital, a nice remuneration for doing it, oodles of praise, and always a slice of jam sandwich and some home-made lemonade

from old Mrs Bugler. Helen was a clip. They would
puncture her bicycle, cut and shave her hair while she
slept soundly, throw kettles of boiling water over her
and bury her alive in a grey winding sheet. Mad with
anger Peg sloshed water around the floor, repeated her
wicked plans and then for fear of reprisal they both
knelt down to mop it up, and Creena said that they
ought to offer up their hunger in the hope that their
father would come home sober and their mother have
an enjoyable time. Then they discussed the presents
and as always the unfairness of their lot. Helen was to
get a dress length, Teddy a tennis racket, Creena a
sleeping doll, and Peg a bottle of lotion to make her
brown as a berry. Peg was in love with the new school
teacher and had spoken on one occasion to him during
which he admitted that he liked sallow skin, and that
raisins in cake happened to be the bane of his life. He
was courting Della, a young butter maker, and each
evening they set out from the town and went towards
the old woods adjoining the hospital, and were never
seen coming home. Peg predicted that it would not
last. That evening they offered their hunger up for
their parents' happiness, their happiness, and happiness in general. The following morning they were
ravenous. The routine was the same – they were sent
by Helen to fetch mushrooms which they gathered,
stewed in peppered milk, ate, and were still ravenous.

In the afternoon when Teddy and Helen had gone
off on their bicycles the two ransacked the house for
anything edible they might find. In vain. The hun-
grier they became the more they envisaged meals –
cakes, fairy cakes, orange cakes, plum cakes, madeira
cakes; warm bread on trays; custards with a beautiful

thin skin on them; boiled bacon soft and juicy and still pink; apples stewed to a warm brown; pears stewed in their own syrup; bowls of potato salad with hard-boiled eggs and scallions added for flavour. They licked their arms, their cardigans, dry plates, the table top, and once again lamenting their hunger went on the prowl. They found a poison letter to their mother, their father's revolver, four orange-coloured cartridges, and a prayer to St Joseph that was supposed never to fail. They said it devotedly, continued their rampage, and found a gold sovereign in their mother's jewellery box, along with the two black rings, the one square, the other oval, rings that they always knew were secretly important to their mother, although she chose never to wear them. Then they thought of going to the shop to secure credit but knew that their father had quarrelled with Tom the very day he left for the horse show. Their father went over to get provisions on credit, Tom refused, their father hit the counter with his ash plant and said that it was as good to have it down in the bloody book than rotting in the bloody sack. Names were thrown at one another, accusations about their father's dreadful drinking, counter accusations about Tom's wife, who was in the lunatic asylum and eventually a sack of grain and a pint of Jeyes Fluid got spilt over the scales.

Next day Tom commissioned the young man who did landscapes to do a large sign which said 'No credit today, all free foodstuffs tomorrow'. Peg said Creena must go, and coax something out of Tom, even porridge, but Creena was in terror, because one day, in fact Good Friday, he had called her into the office, lifted her dress up and touched her under her dress with his handkerchief, and then given her a shilling.

She asked him to deduct the shilling from their out-
standing bill, whereupon he laughed, touched her
again, warned her to tell no one, said if she did she
would be carried off to the Shannon by an evil spirit.
The shilling was long spent on cachoux, a lace-edged
hanky and a candle to atone for whatever the thing was
that had taken place. The only place they were likely
to get anything free was from the new lady in the medi-
cal hall who was always smiling at girls, called Creena
'daughter', stroked her hair, and even once pulled a rib
out to have as a souvenir. Peg said they could at least
get cough lozenges, or better still Vick which they could
put in blobs on the tongue, and hence induce nausea
and defer hunger. Creena said that she would not go,
whereupon Peg threatened to do all the tortures to
Creena that were formerly intended for Helen. She
tied Creena to a chair, blindfolded her, made her draw
the ends of her fingers over the edge of a rusted razor
blade, and made her confess to sins that she had not
committed. She then told her how she would operate
on her, have her bleed to death, whereupon she would
die, go to hell, and never see her own mother again.
Creena began to sniffle, then to cry and then imagining
the deep dungeons of hell and the numbers of mocking
devils, she developed convulsions, started to gasp, and
had to have cold water poured over her and be given
dolls for comfort's sake.

Long after the spate of tears had died down, she was
still drying her tears in the blonde frizzy hair of her
second favourite doll, when Helen returning found
them sitting in the middle of the kitchen, their two
chairs side by side, their arms around one another, sob-
bing, incanting about their hunger, their sad life, and
the fact that their father might come home drunk and

kill them all. Helen was wearing a new silver slide in her hair. She had been given it by Miss Bugler, just as a week before she had been given a bolero, and a brooch the week before that. She asked them did they want to be locked up or were they perhaps rehearsing a Christmas play. Without being told to Creena jumped up and began to sweep the floor. It was almost dark. Peg pinched Creena's leg and then all of a sudden prostrated herself and began to roll and moan like a possessed woman. She started saying good-bye to them, her beloved sisters, said how they would meet at the gates of heaven, said that the warts Helen had had on her cheeks would surely come back, predicted that Creena would go far in the walk of life but would have an unhappy love affair, and would die of a broken heart, in the gutter. Then she rose, and began to float around the kitchen saluting saints, predicting terrible things like drought, distemper for the two dogs, foot and mouth disease; crying out to her earth mother for being so hard, saying she knew where the lost shilling was but that it was irretrievable since fairies had claimed it. She called on the colour purple and spoke some Latin nouns. Then she moaned and writhed and at the very pitch of her performance she fell in a heap on a pile of dust in the middle of the floor. They rushed to her. Helen got the mirror to see if she was breathing and very solemnly Creena told Helen that their dear sister had died of hunger. They hauled her up the stairs to the nearest bed. Helen flew off on her bicycle to get some eats and still exhausted from her great performance Peg opened and closed an eye and gave Creena a wonderful and gratified wink. Hearing a knock Creena went tripping downstairs certain that it was Helen, and there instead, she found in their kitchen, a man with whiskers, gabbling names, wielding a shears, a big old brown rusted shears. She too fainted.

When Helen arrived seconds later she found her two sisters again in a state of hysteria, in the middle of the floor, the dog whelping and the strange man bent in an effort to bring them to their senses. He kept asking which woman's name could be spelt the same backwards or forwards. He explained that he was a travelling man, buying sheep's wool and hence the big brown shears. Helen got rid of him, and immediately knelt down opening a bag to reveal two small round loaves, one with currants and one dusted over with icing sugar. Without even waiting for an implement they broke off big chunks of the bread, blessed it, and ate it, much too quickly. Helen said they would get indigestion.

For the next two days they were allotted two slices of bread each and this was put on their plates in the morning so that they could eat or ration it as they wished.

Their mother and father arrived, their father paralytic and carried by a strange man, and already a sour smell of drink prevailed in the neglected kitchen. Their mother cried, clutched her handkerchief and told of the terrible disgrace in the train, when without a ticket or the wherewithal she had tried to evade the collector by hiding in the lavatory. A gypsy woman was hiding in the other lavatory, but the two of them were called out, apprehended, disgraced, and made to give their full names and addresses. The gypsy woman had the gall to ask her for coppers, which as she said, she did not possess. The ticket collector didn't approach their father who was as it seems vituperative with everyone. They sat and wept. Their mother opened a bit of yellow silk and said it was a remnant, and that there was enough for a dress for Helen and maybe a little bodice for either Peg or Creena, depending on who needed it most.

She was disconsolate and could not drink her tea. Where would the money come from, how were they to live, what trials and tribulations did the future hold? Helen called her out and underneath the pantry window, under the watchful eyes of the other two, Helen took two items from her bodice, a tiny gold wristwatch with a strap of gold mesh and a folded pound note, saved from the housekeeping. The wristwatch had been given her by the Bugler family as a token for all her errands. The money could go towards groceries, their father would sleep it off, the corn was turning, the hens would get the pickings of wheat and surely be inspired to lay.

Her mother kissed her, and said that she was the best and most farseeing little girl, she thought of everyone, and as a reward the two rings upstairs, her only worldly possessions were to be Helen's, and worn any time she liked. They held one another and cried while inside the others cried bitterly and it seemed to Creena that her mother had been misled and grievously mistaken, and would never be her true mother again.

Love-Child

I walked by the river and straightaway fell to thinking of Hickey. The story of the goose was the obvious reason, since he had shot one close to that very spot. Geese cackled from the opposite bank, their cackles muted somewhat and almost melodious because of being issued through a fine growth of rushes. He came to mind clearly in his plus-fours, with his big appetite and his thieving. All our own geese had been taken by a fox one year, but directly across the river dwelt a family who had a fine flock and he resolved to shoot one. He did it at dusk, but it so happened that the goose he shot was a wild goose, with scarcely a lick of meat on it, and my mother was boiling and broiling it for four days to no avail. Even the broth was insipid.

I think it was to make up for that fiasco that he stole the cabbages. My mother came down to breakfast one morning to find a sack full of York cabbages on the floor, and though Hickey wouldn't admit it, my mother knew he had filched them from Mrs Minogue's garden, She was the old woman with a little plot of ground behind the sweetshop. The only woman whose cabbages had not been consumed by slugs that year. Later in the day, my mother gasped to see old Mrs Minogue hurrying up the drive with a bundle held in front of her. The sack of cabbages was hidden in the shoe closet, where I think it contracted a permanent smell of must, and my mother was busy concocting excuses when Mrs Minogue knocked both on the window and on the door, as country people tend to do. She refused to come in, being too shy, but out of her apron she dropped four heads of cabbage, starting crying, and said it nearly broke her heart to have only four to give to us. She then told how some blackguard had robbed her during the night – said it must have been a tinker – and she went off hurriedly, muttering apologies about not being able to offer better. My mother never tasted any of those cabbages, and Hickey grew well and truly tired of them; like me, he maintained that the odours and sweat of the shoe closet had permanently impaired them.

The next thing he stole was a sword from the General's grave, directly after the General's burial, and a very fearsome affair it was in its leather scabbard. He boasted how he could have stolen a watch or a medal from the same source but that it was only weapons he was after. He kept it under his bed, along with sundry things like bicycle chains, pedals, and odd bits of scrap metal.

He stole from us, too, and the day he was leaving my mother asked him to kindly return the little teaspoon to make up the dozen, because there was a terrible gap in her velvet-lined box – a spoon-shaped gap where the missing spoon should be. He denied taking it, but afterwards we found the spoon on the cow-house window, stained yellow to make it seem that he had been using it for dosing cattle. We couldn't afford to pay him, so he went to England to take up work in a car factory. We heard that he kept up his agricultural skills and had an allotment, which served both as a pastime and as a means of earning extra money. We heard from a neighbour who worked in the same factory and who came home to his mad wife for three months of each year and begot another soft-headed child. It seemed that Hickey was prospering.

Whenever Hickey was mentioned, the same stories were told. He had been invited to a wedding and announced to my father that he wouldn't be available for milking on a certain day. He rose early, cooked himself three rashers and two eggs, and wakened everyone with his humming, so jubilant was he. The egg-shells askew on the table galled my mother, as did the dinner plate with the thick lodge of fat on it. He waited down at the wicker gate, probably whistling, thinking ahead to the largesse – the eighteen bottles of whiskey, ditto of brandy, champagne, and barrels of porter. He had heard the groom order from the publican the evening before, and even he was obliged to say perhaps it was too extravagant. The wedding was to be held some miles away in a lakeside town, where the couple had rented a banqueting suite. The lake and pleasure boats would provide an added excitement – as the groom said, it was more of an event to go elsewhere for a wedding than to stay at home.

Hickey waited seven hours in all, pacing back and forth, lighting a cigarette and then putting it out only to light it again and finally spit out the tobacco. The neighbour who obliged by taking the milk to the creamery said Hickey's nerves were a devil altogether – that he was like a jumping jack down there, or a flea in a matchbox. It was long past lunchtime when the postman told him how they had been fooling him – there was no wedding at all, and the big order of whiskey and porter was given only to substantiate the joke. Hickey was lepping. He came up home, went to bed, and refused to eat or speak, or do the evening milking.

The other story concerned a servant girl, Rosanna, who was six months' pregnant, and how the doctor, who was also her employer, came to Hickey in the cornfield and told him that he was responsible. Hickey denied it, lost his head, and raised the pitchfork to the doctor, who escaped only because he was such a practised runner and very fit.

Soon after, Hickey left. I cried for several weeks and used to stay in his room, standing by the little window in order to smell him, feel him, hear him, in order to commune with him. Often I saw his tongue travelling over his verdigris teeth, and so many times saw his big frame come in at the gate below, and saw him run a few steps to work up the thrust to get his leg over the bar of his bicycle. Saw him as clearly as if he had been approaching, but in fact never saw him again.

He did come back to the neighbourhood one summer. He went to see his friend the publican, and although intending to come and pay us a visit he got drunk and was sent home stretched out in the back of a lorry. My mother took it badly, wondering why he had behaved so spiteful, saying England had ruined him, but I myself, still loving him, thought that perhaps our house and the driveway and his own little room, converted now into a bathroom, would sadden him and revive too many memories – the summers, the harvest, the threshing, the little ferret he had, the time he had fallen asleep down in the woods when supposed to be watching for foxes, the way he was scandalized in the local paper by having a skit written about him: 'Gunman Snores While Mr Reynard Steals Farmer's Fowl'. Also, in my most secret thoughts it occurred to me that his fury with the doctor must have meant he was responsible. There was no way of telling, because the maid had slept with everyone – the local men from the cottages whose wives were dead or having babies or in the asylum; the circus people who came a couple of times a year; the black doctor; in fact, anyone, and hence she was called the Bicycle.

At any rate, we never heard a word of Hickey until two days after my walk by the river, when the news came of his death. He died at fifty-seven after a long illness, had lost three stone, and was buried overseas.

I did what I had postponed doing for years. I made the journey to the factory town in England where he worked and to the house where he had lived with his sister. It was a small terraced house on a hill, adjacent to the country, and inside sat an invalid who I imagined was a cousin of his. She looked both very old and very young, and her little hands were like a china doll's; I shuddered at shaking one of them. I have never seen a creature whose eyes moved so much. They literally danced in her head, and I decided that, because of her inactivity otherwise, she must have over-developed these eye muscles to do her travelling for her.

There were various ornaments in the room, too, that stirred or rattled or chimed, and coloured liquid in a glass tube that constantly kept trickling into different shapes creating different formations. As if that were not enough, there were birds in cages – canaries all busy, twittering and agitating and singing. His sister told me that Hickey had bought them and trained them to sing, and even left their cage doors open to let them taste their freedom. She added that after his death the canaries also went silent.

She insisted on showing me his bedroom. It was a cheerless little room, with a patch of damp on the flowered wallpaper; the window looked out onto the hill behind. She gave me his mortuary card and I read the verse about ashes and dust, and she stood watching and sniffling, and then for want of something to do she spread her hand over the satin coverlet to smooth it, although it was not in need of smoothing, and she was telling me, almost against my will of his last days and the way he raved about our house and the bog, and his old friends, and how he was trying to get cabbages to them, and then she listed off the names of all the people; my mother, my father, the doctor, Rosanna the maid, Jacksie his friend, the publican, my sisters – especially my sisters. There was not a word about me. I asked. 'He never mentioned you.' I said that was impossible, since I was his favourite, since he was in the house at my birth, since he taught me the time and boiled pullet's eggs for me, and brought me to hurling matches and often gave me Turkish delight. I lost my head, rather, and related some of our daft prattle and our promises to wed one day.

She lit into me, lost her composure, saying he never forgave me – saying she would never forgive me, either – because it was my fault he had stayed so long in our house and for little or no remuneration. Wasted himself out of love for me. Converted me into the daughter he never had, could never afford to have. My fault that he hadn't told the truth! It seems the creature downstairs was his daughter, the love-child, whom he had sought out and taken from the orphanage in London where her mother had put her.

I wanted to cry out to say love puts ridiculous bonds on people, I wanted to go downstairs and look into her

133

eyes and see if they were a shiny periwinkle grey like his, but instead of that I ran out of there clutching the mortuary card, rebuking him for having been so feeble as to hide from us, from me, the truth, and all the love that he had borne me seemed no more than a ridiculous pretence. As ridiculous as the second verse on the mortuary card that said, 'A devout life came to an end. He died as he lived, everyone's friend.' A sham of a life. No one's friend. I cursed him. I dared him to speak up for himself. But it is not good to repudiate the dead because then they do not leave you alone, they are like dogs that bark intermittently at night.

The House of my Dreams

She hurried home from the neighbour's house to have a few spare moments to herself. The rooms were stripped, the windows bare, the dust and the disrepair of the ledges totally revealed, everything gone except for the few things she insisted on taking herself – a geranium, a ewer, and a few little china coffee cups that miraculously had escaped being broken. There was a broom against the wall – a soft green twig that scarcely grazed the floor or penetrated to the rubble adhering there. Neighbours were good the day one moved house. No, that was not fair. She had had good neighbours, and a variety of them. She had spent nights with them, got drunk with some of them, slept with one of them, and later regretted it, quarrelled with one of them, and with another had made a definite plan to have a walk in the country, once a week, but excuses always intervened, hers and the woman's.

She went to the children's room and hollered 'Hey round the corner po-po, waiting for Henry Lee.' This was the room where nightly, her children used to squabble over who would have the top bunk, and where she brought cups of hot milk, thick with honey, for the colds and congestions they did not have, and where her elder son used to enjoy looking up at the skylight, listening to the rain go pitter-patter, hoping for the snow to fall, listening (though one cannot hear it) to the sun coming up and lighting the pane of glass, watching the gradual change from dark sheet to transparent sheet, and then to a resemblance of something dipped in a quick wash of bright morning gold. Her son had dreamt that there were pink flamingoes in a glass, a glass that he was drinking from, and that they were there because of a special bacteria in the water. That pink, or rather those multiples of feathered pink, layer upon layer, could compare with no colour that he had ever seen. He feasted on it.

The room was empty except for the marks of casters, the initial J. daubed on the wall, and the various stains. When she repeated 'Hey round the corner, po-po', there was not the slightest hint of an echo. Ah yes! The children had ritually buried a coin under one of the loose floor-boards, and no doubt it was down there, somewhere; in its hole, covered in dust and maybe smeared with cobweb.

The night she had served their father with a custody writ, she had gone all around the house, and lifted off the telephones, and watched them where they lay, somehow like numbed animals, black things or white things, or a red thing, that had gone temporarily dead. In the middle of the night her husband came and slipped the threatening letter in under the hall door (she had nailed down the letter box), and she was there cowering and waiting for it, the letter saying, 'They are mine, they are not yours, you are going to be a nervous corpse if you take this to court, you gain nothing except your gross humiliation, you are bound to lose, I cannot show you any mercy, I am really determined to do everything within the law to get custody of those children, no holds barred.' She had read it and re-read it and wrung her hands and wondered how she could have married such a man.

Another time she had waited in the hall, being too shy to stand at the window and at intervals had pushed the letter box open to peep out into space. She was waiting for a man who did not appear. They happened to have the same birthday and that factor along with his smile, made her think somehow he would come, and listening for the car or the taxis she had found herself in a particular stance, a stance repeated from long ago, waiting behind a window in a flannel nightgown for a man, her father, who anyhow might thrash her to death. It was as if all those past states only begged to be repeated, to be relieved, to go on for ever and ever, amen. Those things were like shackles that bound her.

The house had been her fortress. And yet there were snags. The time when a total stranger knocked, a tall thin man, asking if he could have a word with her, stepping inside on to the rubber mat and telling her that he had no intention of leaving her alone. It happened to be late spring, and he was framed by the hawthorn tree and looking at it, and the soft nearly-emergent petals she thought 'If I pretend not to be in the least bit afraid, he will go away.' That was what she did – stared at the tree, giving the impression that someone else was in the house, that she was not petrified, that she was not stranded, not alone. He repeated his intention, then she dismissed him saying, 'We will see about that' and she closed the door very quietly. But back in the house she began to tremble and was too incapacitated even to lift the telephone to call anyone, then when she heard his footsteps go away, she lay down on the floor and wondered why it was that she could not have talked to him, but she knew why it was, because she was petrified of such people. They were usually fanatical, they had a funny stare, and they laughed at things that were no laughing stock. The first such person she had ever come across had been a woman, a tall streelish creature whose mania gave her a wild energy, made her stalk fields, roads, by-roads, lanes, made her rap on people's doors at all hours of day and night, insult them about their jobs, their self-importance, their furniture and everything that they had taken to be enhancing. She could not have appeared casual for fear he might strangle her, or misbehave, treat the floor as a lavatory, or worse, split her head off. She had the glass changed, so that she was enabled to see out but no caller could see in. He came a few times but was told to scarper by a builder, who was in her employment.

It had been a nice lunch, delicate – poached eggs and leaf spinach. When she sat down the neighbour handed her a linen napkin and said 'There you are pet.' They drank wine, they clinked glasses, they recalled Christmases, numerous parties, the Scottish boy whom they both fancied and deceived each other over. At the time it had rankled. She herself had met him on the road one morning, by the merest chance, and he had the temerity to tell her he had been looking for a hardware shop although it was a street solely of private houses. But that was well behind her. The garden would go on blooming. The Virginia creeper would attach itself to everything and finally encumber everything. She had put down three trees, numerous creepers, herbs and wonderful bright shrubs that defied the nourishless

London soil. She would recall the garden in times to come, the evenings sitting out on the low wall, looking at the river, or again at the blocks of flats on the opposite side, feeling the vibrations of the distant tube train go right through her stomach and her bowels, admiring the flowers, and sometimes getting down to stake up a rose that had straggled and bowed along the ground. It had been a home. 'No place like home' her parents used to say whenever they went away from their ramshackle farm, to be ill, or to shop for a day, or in the case of her father to go on binges.

She went up to her bedroom. Nothing left of its character but the wallpaper. Beige wallpaper with bosses of red roses, each rose like an embryo bud, and all intricately joined by stems that were as thin as thread, and on the point of ravelling. Not many people had seen her bedroom, but those who had, were still in it like ghosts, spectres, frozen in the positions that they had once unthinkingly occupied. There was a boy, blond, freckled, who had never made love to her, but had harboured some true feelings for her. He used to always arrive with a group but almost always got too drunk to go home, and once though not drunk, felt disinclined to go home and took off his boots by the fire, and held the soles of his feet towards it, asking if by any chance seers read feet, if feet had lines of destiny just like hands. She thought that maybe shyness had deterred him, or maybe distaste. He used to talk in the early morning, the very early morning, touching the stems of the roses with his forefinger, watching the careens of the birds through the window, and the course of the river beyond. People used to envy her that view of the river. Yes it was a shame to leave. At night because of the aspect of the water and its lap, it often seemed as if it were another city altogether, and now just as the trees were beginning to grow she was leaving it all behind. She ought to desecrate it, do some misdeed, such as at school when they got holidays and used to throw compasses and chalk about, used to chant 'Kick up tables, kick up chairs, kick Sister so-and-so down the stairs, no more Latin, no more French, no more sitting on a hard old bench.' But those were the carefree days, or seemed to be.

'I am loathe to leave' she thought, and dragged the broom over the bare wood floor. Dust rose out of nowhere, so she filled a coffee cup with water and spattered it over the floor to keep the motes down. Once, during a very special party she thought that the freckled boy must not be coming, and then just as her hopes were dashed, he arrived with a new girl, a girl not unlike herself, but younger, tougher and more self-assured. The girl had asked for cigars immediately, and strode around the room smoking a cigar, telling all the men that she knew they lusted after her. She was both clever and revolting. At the end of the night there was only the three of them left and they sat in a little huddle. He was right in the throes of a sentence, when all of a sudden he fell fast asleep, the way children do, leaving the two of them to watch over him, which they did like vultures. Together they removed his high boots, his suède jacket, and his outer sweater. When at last the girl fell asleep, she herself went around her own house, stacking glasses, thinking it had been a good party, primarily because he was there. And occasionally, even in those very early days things would suddenly become otherwise, and her heart would enter on a disaster. She would forget a name, even her own name, or a cigarette butt in a glass would be enlarged a hundredfold, and once the violets came out of a brooch and it seemed to her they were exuding either sweat or tears. The cheeky girl rang her employer the moment she wakened, and asked how Kafka, her dog, was. Then she borrowed money and walking away from him with a strut, said 'Isn't he chubby,' his function in her life now completed.

The children used to have parties too, birthday parties, where all the glasses of diluted orange would be lined up on the tray, and the piles of paper hats towered into a cone; and later meringue crumbs would be sent flying about the place and some children would be found crying because they had not gone to the lavatory. It was worst when they left to go away to boarding school – empty rooms, empty beds, and two bicycles just lying there in the shed. They would come home for holidays and there would be the usual bustle again, various garments left on the various steps of the stairs, but it was always as if they were visitors, and gradually the house began to have something of the chilliness of a tomb.

But she met the holy man, and having talked to him at length, and hearing his creed she asked him to join her, to come under her roof. The very first evening, however, she had a premonition, because arriving as he did at the appointed hour, and with his rucksack, she saw that he had a black scarf draped over his head, and catching sight of him in the doorway he looked like nothing so much as a harlot his Asiatic features sharply defined, his eyes like darts and full of expectation. They sat by the fire, she served the casserole, bringing

a little table close for him to balance his plate on. He
even drank some wine. He told her of his daydream to
go by boat down the French canals, throughout the
length of a summer. When the time came to retire it
seemed to her that he let out some sort of whimper.

Once in her bedroom she locked her door and began
to tremble. She had just embarked on another catastrophe. On his way to bed he coughed loudly, and it
seemed to her that he lingered on the landing, just
outside her door. She was inside, cringing, listening.
She seemed to be always listening, cringing, in some
bed, or under some bed, or behind some pile of furniture, or behind a door that was weighed down with
overcoats and trench-coats. She seemed to be always the
culprit, although in truth the other person was the
killer.

In the morning the holy man slipped a note under
her bedroom door, to say she was to join him the
moment she wakened, as they did not want to lose a
moment of their precious time together. She greeted
him coldly in the kitchen, but already she could see
that he was hanging on her words, on her looks, and on
her every gesture. After three days it was intolerable.
His sighs filled the house, and the rooms that were
tolerably cheerful with flowers and pretty objects,
these too began to accumulate a sadness. She found herself hiding, anywhere, in the lavatory, in the garden
shed, in the park, even though it was bitter cold. He
would rush with a towel and slippers whenever she
came in and had some mush ready, which he insisted
she eat. He called her 'angel' and used this endearment
at every possible moment. The neighbours said he
would have to go. She knew he would have to go.

The day she told him he said it was his greatest fear

realized, that of becoming happy at long last – his wife had died ten years before – only to be robbed of it. He broke down, said how he had dreamed of bringing her up the French canals, of buoying her with cushions so that she could see the countryside, loving her, and caring for her and lulling her to sleep.

On the day of his departure he wrote a note, saying that he would stay in his room, his 'hole' as he called it, and not bother her, and not require any food, and leave quietly at four as arranged. At lunchtime she called him to partake of a soup she had made. He was in his saffron robe, all neat and groomed, like a man about to set out on a journey. But he was shivering, and his eyes had a veil over them, a heavy veil of tears. He sat and dragged the spoon through the thick potato soup, and at first she thought that it must be some way of cooling it, but as the time went by she saw that it was merely a ploy to fiddle with it, like a child.

He did not say a word. She clapped her hands and much too raucously, said 'High diddle diddle the cat and the fiddle the cow jumped over the moon. The little dog laughed to see such sport and the dish ran away with the spoon.' He looked at her as if she had gone mad. She said 'Please don't take it so badly.' He said she was the second person he had ever loved, said how his wife had been a European too, sired in a dark wet country, a lover of rain and a lover of music. He loved nothing Asiatic, nothing related to his own land, not even the sunshine or the bright colours or the smells that pervaded the air of Bombay. His destiny was his dead wife, and now her.

Anger overtook her so that she wanted to beat him with the spoon, grind his face into the mush of soup, she wanted to humiliate him. When she was clearing away the dishes, he said again that he would stay in his 'hole' and leave quietly at four. But when the clock struck she waited for his footsteps on the stairs, and then along the hall, but she waited in vain. She prayed to God that he would go.

At five she decided that he must have killed himself, and before going up, she took the precaution to call in the neighbour. Together they climbed the stairs, smoking vigorously, manifesting a display of courage. He was sitting in the middle of the floor with his rucksack on, his head lowered. He appeared to be praying. He said 'Angel' and how he must have lost track of time. Then he said it was too late to go, and that he would postpone his departure until the morrow.

Eventually she had to call the police, and upon leaving he handed her a note which said that he would never get in touch with her, never ever, but telling her where he would be at each and every given hour. He was taking employment as cook, and he wrote his employer's number, stressing that he would be there at all hours, except when he intended to travel by bus, two afternoons a week, to take guitar lessons. Then he gave her the various possible numbers of the guitarist, who had no fixed abode. Next morning another letter was slipped under the door, and so each morning faithfully until he died seven days later. She refused to admit her guilt.

Soon after she decided to have the renovations done – kitchen and living room made into one, a big picture window, to afford a grander view of the river, and a stained glass window in which a medley of colours could interact as they did in the church windows seen long ago. The cubes and the circles and the slithers of light, that had fascinated her in childhood were still able to repossess her at a moment's flounder. Like the knots, and the waits, and the various sets of chattering teeth. Other things too – shouts, murmurs, screams, an elderly drunk falling down a stair, his corpse later laid out in an off-white monkish habit, on a wrought-iron bed, and she herself being told that he had died of pneumonia, that he had not died of a fall.

So many puzzling things were said, things that contradicted one another. They congratulated you for singing, then told you never to open your gob again as long as you lived. Your tongue was not your friend, it was too thick and unwieldy, it doubled back in your throat, it parched, it longed for lozenges. Yes, rows, and the prefaces to rows, and thumpings and beatings and the rash actions of your sister the flighty one, going out at night, winter night, with blue satin knickers on, which she had stolen, going to a certain gateway, to cavort with a travelling creamery manager, coming in long after midnight, and trying desperately not to be heard, but being heard and accosted fiercely.

For some curious reason creaks are more pronounced in the dark, and her sister was always heard and always badly punished so that there were cries after midnight and don't, don't, don't. Her sister bled on that stair, then soon after her mother, her father, a clergyman and two other important men interrogated her about her private life. Her sister denied everything, just stayed there, glued to the damp area of the stairs. Then the next day, her mother, her sister, and herself walked along a hedged road and every minute her sister was cross-examined, and every minute she denied the accusations and said she was a virgin. They were on their way to another doctor, a doctor who did not know them. When they passed an orchard the little apples were already formed on the trees and they were desperately bright, but hard and inedible. Her sister had been found to have lied – had tried to abort herself, was sent to the Magdalen laundry for the five remaining months and had her bitter confinement there.

But there had been consoling things too – treats. On Sundays a trifle left to set on the other side of the stained glass panel, a trifle in a big pudding bowl, left down on tiles to cool. She would go down the stairs in her nightdress, creep, go through the glass door, squat down on those tiles, and scoop out some of the lovely cold jollop with her hands, and swallow it. It was cakey. Later it would be covered over with a layer of whipped cream then sprinkled with hundreds and thousands which would shine away as they were being swallowed. She never got a walloping for that misdemeanour because in her mother's eyes she was a little mite. On the other hand her father punished her for everything, particularly for sleeping in her mother's bed. When her father got in she tried not to look, not to listen, not to see, not to hear and not to be. She moved over to the wall, smelt the damp of the paper and could even smell the mortar behind the paper. There were mice in that room. They scuttled. Shame, shame, shame. Always for one second, a dreadful swoon used to overwhelm her too. Her bones and every bit of her dissolved. Then she contracted and steadied herself.

After her father went back to his own bed, she and her mother ate the chocolate sweets, little brown buttons. They simply used to melt on the tongue, like Holy Communion. They were so soothing, and so satisfying after the onslaught. Then the worst was over for a week or so, until it happened again.

On one side of the bed was a lattice, and when a finger was put through, it was like a finger being dispatched into space. Fingers alone could do nothing but fingers seamed to knuckles, belonging to palms, to wrists and to arms, could stir cakes or pound potatoes, or shake the living daylights out of someone, out of one's own self. One's lights were in there, residing, not as an illumination but as offal. Lights that were given to dogs, to curs and did not show the way as did a lamp or a lantern.

Saturday mornings were languor time. Her mother brought her tea and fingers of toast. The sun would be streaming through the blind, making shapes and gestures, warming the weeping, historied walls, the dark linoleum would be lit up, the dust rambling all over it, the dust an amusement in itself, while out on the landing the sun beamed through a stained glass window resulting in a different pattern altogether. Happily she munched on those fingers of toast. Even the stone hot water bottle that had gone cold became a source of pleasure, as she pressed on it with her feet, and pushed it right down to the rungs of the brass bed and threatened to eject it. When her father threatened her with the slash hook her nostrils went out like angels' wings, and she sped with the prodigal speed over three marsh fields, to a neighbour's house, to one of the cottagers who was stirring damson jam, while at the same time giving her husband a bath in the aluminium tub. They laughed at her because of the way she shook and asked if perhaps she had seen the banshee.

'No pet, no one can help you, you can only help yourself,' the neighbour had just said. Was that true? Would that always be true?

*   *   *

She went into her empty bathroom. The woodwork was as new and blond as in a showroom, and the bar of almond-shaped soap hanging from the tap asked to be used. She whispered things. She looked at the shower, its beautiful blue trough and the glass-fronted door. They had taken a shower together, she and a new man, a hulky fellow. She hung his shirt over the glass door to serve as a sort of screen. She came and came. He was so good-looking, and so heavy, and so warm, and so urgent, as he pressed upon her that she thought she might burst, like fruit. It was such a pity that he turned out to be crass. 'Let's get married,' he said at once.

She brought him to Paris, and in the hotel room he made himself at home, threw his belongings about, started to swagger, ordered the most expensive champagne, and booked two long-distance telephone calls. Her children were in the adjoining suite. They had not wanted him to come, but remembering the pleasure in the shower, that full knob of flesh inside her, truer, more persuasive than words or deeds, the scalding half happiness, she had let him accompany them, knowing she could not afford it, knowing that he would cadge. The moment he used her toothbrush she knew. She went out to the chemist to buy another, and he said what a pity that she hadn't bought him some after-shave.

She could not sleep with him again. She went down, and reserved another room for him, a cheaper room. They quarrelled disgracefully. He picked up the telephone and asked the telephonist would she like him to come down and fuck her. He said he was 'bad news' but that bad news travelled like wildfire. He moved to the other room but would not leave them alone. He followed them wherever they went and hence the visit was ruined. He rang her saying he was a health officer and had to look at her cunt. He ordered the costliest wines from the cellars and she was certain he would steal furniture or linen. It was a beautiful hotel with circular rooms, and little separated balconies on each landing, affording a view into the well of the hall. The bathroom was like a sitting room, with even a chaise for lying on, and the walls were a lovely warm pink. It was a dry paint, like a powder, and the walls were warm to nestle against. She sat on the chaise and very formally cursed him.

In the maid's room she stood over the wash basin. That was one room she had neglected. The wash basin was an eyesore. Would the new people have it mended, or have it removed. The new owner was a doctor, and there would be a sign chalked up on the pavement saying 'Doctor – in constant use'. The Spanish maid had been a nice girl, but a slut. She used to do old-fashioned things like plait her hair at night, or press her clothes by putting them under the mattress. They used to talk a lot, were chatter-boxes. The first day the maid arrived was in January, and the children were playing snowballs, and had just acquired a new dog. The new dog left little piddles all over the floor, tiny yellow piddles, no bigger than a capsule, and the dinner was specially special because of the new girl, and the children were as bright as cherries, what with the exercize and having been pasted with snowballs, and the excitement of a new dog.

The girl had had a mad father who broke clocks, and a mother who pampered her. She came from a small town in the north of Spain, where there was nothing to do in the evenings, except go for a walk with other girls. The girl ironed her hair to straighten it, and took camomile tisane for her headaches. They exchanged dreams. In the mornings she used to go to the girl's room, sit at the foot of the bed, and take a long time deciding what she should wear that day.

The girl began to dream in English, dreamt of cats, shoals of cats, coming through the window, miaowing, and of herself trying to get the latch closed, trying to push them back. The girl got spoiled, stayed in bed three or four certain days of each month, left banana skins under her pillow, neglected her laundry, and never took the hairs out of her brush or comb. Eventually she had to go. Another parting. So also the little dog, because although house-trained, he developed a nervous disease which made him whine all the time even in sleep, and made him grit his little teeth and grind them, and grind most things.

It was not long after, that something began to go awry. She got the first sniff of it, like a foretaste, and it was a sniff as of blood freshly drawn. Yet it was nothing. Naturally there was a space where the small bay window had been. The builder had hung a strip of sacking there but she was certain something would come through, not simply a burglar, or wind, or rain, but some catastrophe, some unknown, a beast of prey. Whenever she entered that room she felt that something had just vacated it. A wolf she thought. It made people laugh. 'A wolf,' they said, 'the proverbial big bad wolf.' She rummaged through her old books for a copy of *Red Riding Hood*, but could not find it. She could remember it. It was a cloth book with serrated edges. The edges were cut carefully, so that the book did not ravel. She saw the little specks of cloth that had been ripped out, in a heap on the floor, coloured like confetti.

When the big new window was delivered, that hall door had to be taken off its hinges. Six men carried it through, each one bossing the other, telling the other to get a move on, to move on for Christ's sake, to do this, to do that, to watch it, watch it. She saw it break into smithereens a hundred times over, but it wasn't in fact until it was in, and well puttied, that she realized what a risk they had taken. She opened a bottle of whiskey, and they drank, looking out at the river, that happened on that day to have the sheen and consistency of liquid paraffin. It was like a bright skin over the brown water. She imagined spoons of it being donated to loads of constipated tourists who went by on the pleasure boats.

Naturally there was a party to christen the room. Would that have been the time that he brought the insolent girl, who had a dog called Kafka, or was that another time? They were all jumbled together, those parties, those times, like the dishes stacked on the long refectory table, or the bottles of wine, or the damp gold champagne labels, or the beautiful entrées. Perfection and waste.

She placed two men together, whereupon one took offence thinking he was assumed to be a homosexual. She had to bring him out into the garden, and in the moonlight solemnly tell him that she had not been sensitive, that she was a careless, a bad hostess. He was full of umbrage. He said he should not have come. She knew that he would never be invited again. A foreign woman stayed on, and they drank a bit, and picked at the food and drank more, and lay down on the mat by the dying fire. Even the embers were grey. She puffed on it and slowly one coal came to life, then another. Without thinking about it, she began to caress the woman and soon realized that she was well on the way to seducing her.

It was a strange sensation, as if touching gauze, or some substance that was about to vanish into thin air. Like the clocks of dandelions that were and then were not, fugitive dandelions vanishing, running away, everything running away, everything escaping its former state.

The woman asked her to go on, to please go on. She thought of other loves, other touches, and it was as if all these things were getting added together in her, like numbers, being totted up in a vast cash register, poor numbers that would never be able to be separated.

She did go on, and then her own eyes swam in her head, and for no reason she recalled the transparent paper that her mother used to apply to the lower halves of window panes, paper with patterns of butter-flies, and the consistency of water, when dampened. They were both wet. Her fingers inside the woman would leave a tell-tale for all time.

They didn't know what to say. The woman spoke about her chap, what a regular maniac he was. Then the woman told her some facts, about her sordid child-hood in Cairo, about being a little girl, constantly raped by uncles and cousins, and great uncles, and great-great uncles, and with each similar revelation she would say 'horrible eh, horrible eh'.

The woman had lived through wars, had half starved, had eaten cactus root, had been bruised and beaten by soldiers, and hideous though these events were they had not made her deep, or brave, they had not penetrated to her. She was like any other woman at the tail-end of a party, a little drunk, a little fatigued, soured about her fate.

The little dog bared his eye teeth at them. He knew he was being put down, before it happened, hence bit doors, wainscotting, and the legs of chairs, bit avidly in anticipation of his fate. She hadn't told the children until it was over. They cried. Then they forgot.

But did they forget? They too had brimming hearts. Children's hearts broke but they did not know that for a long time. One day they discovered it, and then it was as if some part of them had been removed unthinkingly, on a ritual operating table.

Soon after that she caught the illness, or rather it descended on her, an escalating fever. It centred in the throat, the nose and behind the eyes, and everything about her felt raw. The neighbour used to come to see her, bring Bovril in a thermos, and the doctor came twice a day. But when they were gone it used to possess her again, that look of terror. Would her heart be plucked out of her body, would the roof fall in, would a rat come out of its hiding. She often saw one, on the head of the bed, on the bedknob, poised, bristling.

A girl she'd known had had a rat in her bedroom that got killed by a cat, after hours and hours of play, and had witnessed the last screeching tussle, the leaps, then described the remains – a little heart of dry triangular flesh and a string which was the tail. The girl had found a nice bloke and moved with him into his barge. The very day the girl saw him she wrote him a note saying no person, animal, insect, or thing, had sniffed about her sex for almost a year and asked were there any offers. They clicked.

*   *   *

At the height of the fever, small flying creatures assembled and performed a medieval drama. They flew from the ceiling, perched on the various big brass curtain rings, hid in the dusty hollow space above the wardrobe, and hissed at one another; hiss-hiss. They chattered in a rich and barbarous language. She could comprehend it, though she could not speak it. They stripped her, bare. They worked in pairs, sometimes like angels, sometimes like little imps. They too had tails. They worked quickly, everything was quick and preordained.

She lay prostrate. Her nipples were like two aching mouths, unable to beseech. The Leader, half man, half woman, lay upon her and in that unfamiliar, mocking, rocking copulation, all strength seemed to be sucked out of her. Her nipples had nothing left to give. After milk came blood, and after blood, lymph. Her seducer, though light as a proverbial feather had one long black curved whisker, jutting from his left nostril, and there was no part of her body that did not come under the impact of its maddening trail. The others kept up some kind of screeching chorus. She was wrung dry.

She came to on the floor. She saw the pictures, and her oval, silver-backed mirror, as if she had been away on a long long journey and she resaluted them. In the silence there was a heaviness, as of something snoring, and various hairs had got into the glass of orange juice beside the bed.

The next day when the temperature had abated somewhat, she decided to get a grip on herself, to find the use of her legs again, and to walk around. There was even a walking stick that someone had left behind. She opened a door that led into a room, a little vacant room as it happened, but it was no longer empty, she saw numbers of coffins, throughout the room, lifting and flying about, and she heard a saw cutting through wood, slowly and obstinately.

'Good God, I am dying,' she thought, as the coffins careened about, and then she closed the door and then opened it again, and the room was as it should be, with a single bed, covered in an orange counterpane, a lamp with a white globe, a buckled dressing table, and a painting that represented a very purring heart.

That was the first time. Not long after, the wash-basin in the maid's room took a little dance, and the enamel was like a meal inside her mouth, crushing her teeth. They said it was bad to be alone. It was.

She lost interest in cooking and housekeeping, wagged her finger at her own self, and pronounced a ridiculous verdict, 'You are slipping, slipping.' Very often she caught sight of a bright sixpence concealed inside a wad of dough, and she thought that if she could get it, and keep it in her purse, it would be a good augury for the future. Yes, she was slipping. Her hardworking mother would not approve. Her mother had been a good cook, superb at puddings, blood puddings, suet puddings, and of course the doyen of all, the inimitable Queen of puddings.

The neighbours suggested she take driving lessons, and she did. On the very second lesson, she headed straight for a pond, escaped only because the instructor grabbed the steering wheel. All she could hear was 'The pond, the pond.' She saw it, with its fine fuzz of green scum, looking exceedingly calm and undangerous. The instructor drove home.

She went to a boy called Pierre, to have streaks and highlighting. Consequently, her hair at night suggested the lights of an Aladdin's cave. She should have street-walked. She got a new outfit. She got new boots. They were the colour of hessian and thickly crusted with threaded flowers. In the shop, the male assistant told her that their consultant psychiatrist could tell any woman's character from the footwear she chose. For that she smirked.

There was only one tune in her head, and it was that London Bridge was falling down, falling down. She would sit far back into a chair and try and keep still. But very often it would come, this mutiny, and there was no knowing what blood battles, what carnivals, what mad eyes and bulbous eyeballs would swim before her. Get thee to a nunnery, she said to them in vain. The bills poured in. Nevertheless, she bought unnecessary things, an ivory inlaid occasional table, a rocking chair.

The chair had to stay in the shop window for three days, until a dexterous man came to haul it out. She used to go up to the shop and look at it, observe the word 'Sold' in bold red letters and her name just beneath it. She envisaged sitting on it, going rock a bye baby. She never did, because it had to go back to the shop, still with its corrugated wrapping on it since the cheque had bounced.

She had stopped work supposedly for a month, but by then it was several months. She had been replaced by a younger girl and the column that used to carry her name and her oval-faced likeness each Tuesday morning now had a cute little photograph of a blonde lady, who used the pseudonym of Sappho. Her former editor wrote and said if he could ever do anything for her, he would be only too glad to help. It was both touching and useless.

As time went on she was selling instead of buying. Her dresses, both chiffon affairs, in beautiful airy designs, were in a shop window not far away, and her fox cape had been snatched up in two minutes after she had deposited it, in the second-hand market. She saw the new owner go out in it, strutting, and she wanted to stab her. The new owner wore red platform shoes and she herself made a note to procure a pair when her ship came home.

The children guessed but never said. They got little presents for her – usually nice notebooks and biros to try and coax her back to work. From school they wrote insouciant notes – how they were out of socks, they were almost out of underwear, they wondered if she'd had the leak fixed. A man whom she'd met in the park, another nutter, drew her a graph of her waning sexuality, and presented her with a sealed letter. He wrote:

> It appears you do not appreciate a mature
> person, such as myself, you know many
> cultured children, some you worship, and
> some you ridicule, but dear friend, you say you
> are very occupied, so is The Pope, The United
> Nations, The Brotherhood of Workers, The
> Black Militants, The White Pacifists; all
> playing similar games.
> Fellow puppet of nature, from outside,
> stationed in my space, time, and tranquillity, I
> observe the stardust drifting and pulsating
> through the Milky Way. Good-bye. It is not
> the end of me.

Then he told her to beware. All because she stood him up one day on a park bench, where he was going anyhow, for his afternoon ration of fresh air.

She let the bills come and then dropped them into

the boiler. She was glad she had not converted to oil, otherwise there would have been no boiler, and no ashes, and no ash pan with its lovely big surreal clinkers. The house was silent, and yet in those silences she would hear a little gong, summoning her to something, to prayer perhaps, and then the voices real and imagined, were like packing needles, being dispatched in one ear and out the other, through the brawn of her head. Yet no one had died, not even her parents so that there was no excuse for those ridiculous coffins.

Still morning was morning. She would creep down into the garden, quietly, so that she did not even disturb the pigeons out of their roost, and at once she would be possessed of such a nice feeling, a safeness — talking amicably to the sweetness of nature about her. There were still such things, the milky air, the camellias in their trembling back-drop of shining foliage, which she would smell and touch and inhale, and thank for being there. Symbols of another world, a former world, a beautiful world. What world? Where, when and why had she gone wrong?

It was inside that things were worst. If she sat, or lingered too long in any room, it seemed as if the books, the encyclopedias might commence to talk, the pages might fly open, and reveal something dire. At intervals the walls purred. She was several sizes, tiny and shrinking, holding a doll's stomach, messing, making it say 'ma ma, ba ba', she was beating nettles with a stick, she was squatting under the trees, she was a freak being hoisted up on stilts, she was flying, not flying, fixed frozen. She began to lock the door, on one room after another, and she would listen outside these doors, and peer through their keyholes, but not go in. She locked every room in that house, had a camp bed down in the hall, and was ready to fly at the slightest hint of irregularity. In the end she rented a room in a small hotel, and came home only for a change of clothing, or to collect the mail.

'Knock-knock.' He was there. She went out smiling and he helped her with the few things that she was carrying. He hesitated before pulling on the choke. In the back seat were two cardboard boxes, full of empty milk bottles, and the moment they started up, two or three of the bottles rolled off.

'Any regrets?' Yes, plenty of regrets. She was going to a place named after a lake and she and others would be under supervision. He said she would be all right, that there were plenty others in the same boat. Her hackles did not rise.

Ah, never did the house look so lovely as just then, the sheltering eaves from which the birds were darting in and out, the multi-coloured brick with its hues of violet and crimson, the paintwork, that with a bit of effort could be renewed. She had thrown it all away, she had let it go. Her lungs burst for a moment, with regret, and she thought of the alternative, of how blissful it would be, to be going in there and starting all over again, with wooden spoons and a kitchen table, and a primus or a stove; a few belongings. Then she checked herself. It was no use wishing. She saw the living death and the demons behind her, she saw the sad world that she had invented for herself, but of the future she saw nothing, not even one little godsend.